I,Q SERIES

Book One:
Independence Hall

Book Two:
The White House

Book Three:
Kitty Hawk

PICTURE BOOKS WITH HIS WIFE, MARIE SMITH:

B is for Beaver: An Oregon Alphabet

E is for Evergreen: A Washington State Alphabet

N is for our Nation's Capital: A Washington DC Alphabet

Z is for Zookeeper: A Zoo Alphabet

W is for Waves: An Ocean Alphabet

OTHER NOVELS BY ROLAND SMITH

Storm Runners

Storm Runners: The Surge

Storm Runners: Eruption

The 39 Clues: Shatterproof; Cahills vs. Vespers, Book 4

Tentacles

Elephant Run

Peak

Cryptid Hunters

Zach's Lie

Jack's Run

The Captain's Dog: My Journey with the Lewis and Clark Tribe

Sasquatch

Thunder Cave

Jaguar

The Last Lobo

Legwork (e-book)

I, Q

(Book Three: Kitty Hawk)

Roland Smith

Sleeping Bear Press™

www.IQtheSeries.com

Library of Congress Cataloging-in-Publication Data on file.

ISBN 978-1-58536-604-0
1 3 5 7 9 10 8 6 4 2

ISBN 978-1-58536-605-7 (case)
1 3 5 7 9 10 8 6 4 2

This book was typeset in Berthold Baskerville and Datum
Cover design by Lone Wolf Black Sheep
Cover illustration by Kaylee Cornfield

Printed in the United States.

Sleeping Bear Press

315 E. Eisenhower Parkway, Suite 200
Ann Arbor, Michigan 48108

© 2012 Sleeping Bear Press
visit us at sleepingbearpress.com

For Michael Spradlin. You're it!

SUNDAY, SEPTEMBER 7 >

12:00 a.m. to 1:35 a.m.

The President's Kid

Willingham Culpepper, aka P.K., sat at the head of the long conference table in the Situation Room beneath the West Wing of the White House. He was in his pajamas, robe, and slippers. Sitting next to him was his father, J. R. Culpepper, the president of the United States. He was wearing a suit, but he had taken off his tie. He was scanning a wall of video monitors.

Earlier in the evening, P.K. had been drugged and nearly kidnapped by a group of terrorists that had infiltrated the White House.

"How's your head now?" his father asked, swiveling his chair away from the monitors to look at him.

"Still a little fuzzy, but I'm okay," P.K. said. "What did they give me?"

"I don't know, but it was the same drug they gave your sister."

His older sister Bethany had not been as lucky as P.K. The terrorists had successfully gotten her out of the White House and were now driving down I-95 in a Chevy Tahoe with her, unconscious, in the back.

P.K. looked up at the central video monitor. An unmanned drone was following the Tahoe, streaming live video into the Situation Room.

"I guess I'm confused," P.K. said. "If we know where Bethany is, why don't we send in a hostage rescue team to get her back?"

"We may do just that," his father said. "But not yet. I think she's safe for now. Malak Turner is protecting her."

"Who's Malak Turner?"

"She's an ex-Secret Service agent, who up until tonight I thought was dead. She's infiltrated the terrorist cell and is trying to find out who's in charge of it so we can arrest them."

By *arrest them*, P.K. knew his father meant *kill them*, but he let it go. His father always treated him like he was ten years old, which in fact he was.

"So you know this Malak woman," P.K. said.

"I've known her for years. She was in charge of my protection detail. Bethany knows her too."

"How big is this cell?"

His father shook his head. "We don't know, and that's the problem. They have managed to infiltrate every branch of government, including the White House." He nodded at the Situation Room's locked door. "My staff is on the other side of that door going crazy because I won't let them in. The reason I won't let them in is because I don't know for certain which of them I can trust. Somewhere there's a list of cell members. We need that list, and this is our best chance to get it."

"If Malak has already infiltrated the cell, why does she need Bethany?"

"She's only infiltrated it to a certain level. Bethany is her ticket to the upper echelon of the cell. Someone is in charge. Perhaps more than one person. To get the list, she has to gain their trust. Delivering Bethany will do that. As soon as she meets the head of the cell, Malak will . . . uh . . ."

"Arrest him," P.K. said.

"Right."

"And the SOS team following Bethany doesn't work for the government?"

"No. They're independent contractors."

"And you trust this Tyrone Boone guy and his team?"

"I do. He and his team are about the *only* people I trust at the moment. I've worked with Boone for over thirty years. He's never let me down. But I have taken some other steps just in case things start falling apart, which they often do. For now, Bethany is safe."

A phone on the conference table rang. The president picked it up, listened for a second, then said, "The next person that calls me, or allows a call to come through to me in here, will be fired."

He slammed the phone into the cradle, swiveled his chair back around, and stared at the Chevy Tahoe heading south on I-95.

The Interstate

Hard rain blew sideways across I-95. I looked at my watch. It was midnight.

We were in Virginia heading south. Somewhere in front of us was a Chevy Tahoe. Inside the Tahoe was Secret Service agent Malak Turner, who was supposed to be dead. She was posing as a terrorist known as Anmar, aka the Leopard. She wasn't alone in the Tahoe. A few hours earlier, she had drugged and kidnapped Bethany Culpepper, the president's daughter.

We were all a little tense.

The Sasquatch-sized ex-spy, Felix, was behind the wheel of our parents' luxury motor coach, driving about a hundred miles an hour. Lying next to him in the white-leather passenger seat was Croc, the ancient, almost toothless, mongrel with one blue eye and one brown eye.

Croc was not tense. He was snoring, and drooling, and passing a little gas.

Felix cracked open the window to get some fresh air.

Boone, Angela, and I were sitting at the dining table in the back of the speeding coach, staring at a laptop computer. On the screen was the infrared image of a car traveling exactly seventy miles per hour down the interstate, seventeen miles ahead of us according to the readout in the corner of the screen.

"Slow it down," Boone called up to Felix.

Felix eased his big foot off the gas pedal.

"Why?" Angela asked. "We're miles behind them."

"Spotters," Boone said. "The ghost cell is well organized and extremely paranoid, which is how they've managed to survive all these years. They aren't one step ahead of us, they're ten steps ahead of us."

Angela pointed to the screen. "Right now they're sixteen point five miles ahead of us."

Angela was my brand-new fifteen-year-old stepsister. Two years older than me. (A fact she was constantly reminding me of.) But I'm taller. She was kind of a know-it-all, but I liked her. And she was usually right.

"Spotters?" I asked.

"People sent ahead to see if they're being followed," Angela answered. "It's part of countersurveillance."

Since we'd met Boone, we'd had to learn a new language. I guess Angela was a little more fluent in spy-speak than I was because of her mother, Malak, the woman riding up ahead in the Tahoe with the kidnapped Bethany Culpepper.

"Angela's right," Boone said. "They'll have people stationed along the route watching traffic, maybe even running license plates."

"Hard to do that at seventy miles an hour," I pointed out.

"Not with a point-and-shoot license plate scanner," Boone said.

I looked out the window. Bad luck to get scanning duty on a night like tonight.

"We changed the plates on the coach," Boone continued. "But if they cross-check the plates, they'll see they belong to a Ford Fusion. We'll be busted and the ghosts will vanish."

"Poof," I said.

Boone and Angela didn't laugh. Neither did I. I wasn't joking. There was nothing funny about any of this.

We called the terrorists the ghost cell because we didn't know who they really were or what they called themselves. What we *did* know is that they had just set off two bombs in Washington D.C. that killed or injured dozens of people. But the bombs were just diversions. Their real target had been Bethany Culpepper.

Boone pointed at the speedometer readout at the bottom of the screen, which was still pegged at seventy miles per hour. "Cruise control," he said. "They don't want to risk getting pulled over for speeding."

The video was streaming in from an unmanned drone. Vanessa, one of Boone's SOS team, was flying it from the back of the intellimobile. The president had requisitioned the multimillion-dollar flying bot for our personal use.

SOS was an acronym for Some Old Spooks. The name started out as a joke, but stuck. The team was made up of ex-spies, former black-op military guys, a couple of Israeli Mossad agents, two active Secret Service agents, Angela, and me . . . Q

Munoz, former wannabe magician and rookie terrorist hunter.

The drone was doing a lot more than tracking the car. It was picking up heat signatures from inside it. Four orange blobs. Two in front. Two in back. We figured the two in back were Malak Turner and Bethany Culpepper.

We had no idea who the two in front were.

So Far So Good

Malak Turner looked over at Bethany Culpepper. There was a black hood pulled over Bethany's head—a useless precaution in Malak's opinion. Bethany was unconscious. The drug they had given her at the White House was designed to cause a stupefying sense of euphoria, followed by a coma-like sleep. It would be hours before Bethany woke.

Malak took Bethany's hand and felt her pulse. It was slow, but strong. She had hoped to have Bethany back in the White House long before the effects of the drug wore off, but that was looking more and more unlikely with every passing mile.

Where are we going? she thought. *How long will it take?*

She knew better than to ask the two men in the front seat. To ask would have been a severe violation of cell protocol. And there was a good chance that the men didn't know themselves.

Malak looked at their silhouettes. They hadn't turned around or spoken to her since she had pushed Bethany into the backseat of the Chevy Tahoe two blocks from the White House.

Both men had blinking Bluetooth earpieces in their right ears. They had received several phone calls, but Malak had learned nothing from their one-word replies to whatever they were being asked or told. There was a good chance that the two men had never seen each other before. There was even a better chance that they had no idea that their passengers were the president's daughter and the Leopard. The men had gotten their instructions like all deep-cover cell members. By e-mail. The e-mail would have been simple and vague . . .

I'll meet you on the corner of 15th and H at 7:00 PM. I'm driving the white Chevy Tahoe. I look forward to our outing.

This could be the men's first mission or their tenth. When it was completed, they would return to their family, friends, and jobs as if nothing had ever happened. The cell members came in all shapes, sizes, ages, colors, and genders. They worked in stores, offices, schools, police departments, the military, and government agencies. The one thing they had in common was that they were willing and able to do anything they were asked, without question, regardless of the risk or consequences.

Malak guessed there were hundreds of cell members like the two men in the front seat, but there was only one man who knew the exact number, and who they were. She hoped to meet him before the night was over. Bethany Culpepper was her ticket to the inner circle, but she would cash the ticket in at a moment's notice and throw away everything she had worked for if at any time she thought Bethany would be harmed.

So far so good, she thought and felt her lips arch into a rare smile. It was a punch line to an old joke about an optimist, which she had heard when she was a Secret Service agent. The optimist falls off the Empire State building. As he flies past each floor, bystanders shout out: "How's it going?" He shouts back: "So far so good!"

The driver got a call. He listened, said yes, then ended the call by touching his Bluetooth.

Malak decided to call the driver Willing and the man in the passenger seat Able.

Or better yet . . . Will and Abe.

She smiled again.

Two smiles in a row.

It had been a long time since the Leopard had smiled. She settled back into her seat with her hand on the pistol Abe had given her when she got into the Tahoe.

So far so good.

Off the Books

"Stop shuffling those cards, Quest!"

"What's that, *Angie?*"

"It's Angela."

"It's Q."

"Fine. Stop shuffling, Q. It's driving me crazy."

I stood up, put the cards in my pocket, and started pacing, which isn't easy to do in a swaying motor coach.

Shuffling and manipulating playing cards was about the only thing stopping me from going crazy. Busy hands, my mom calls it. When I get nervous, my hands get busy. If I can't use my hands, my mind gets busy . . .

Until a week ago, my only ambition was to become a famous magician. That's *magician* as in *magic*, not *musician* as in *music*, like my three musician parents. My mom is Blaze Munoz. Exactly a week ago, she married Angela's dad, Roger Tucker. Their single, "Rekindled," is the #1 hit on Billboard. They were supposed to be on a national concert tour, but right now they were sound asleep in the Lincoln Bedroom inside the White House. The president asked them to spend an extra night. He wanted them to do a joint press conference about fund-raising efforts for the victims of the bombings in Washington, D.C. But this was not the real reason they were in D.C. Boone promised Malak that he would protect us *personally*, which would be hard to pull off if he wasn't with us. The president wanted him to go after the terrorists and his daughter. Angela and I were along for the wild ride. Our parents had no idea what was really going on. They thought we were on our way to their next gig. We weren't alone. In addition to the motor coach, there were two other vehicles stalking the Leopard and her prey. Eben Lavi (a rogue Israeli Mossad agent who had stuck a knife in my neck) and Malak's father, Ziv (not his real name), were right behind us in our parents' red Range Rover. Behind them was the intellimobile— the SOS communications surveillance van. Inside the van was a tangle of electronic gear worth more than the 3.5 million-dollar drone. Uly (slightly smaller than Felix, but not by much) was behind the wheel. Vanessa (who was good with a throwing knife) was in the back flying the drone. Next to her was X-Ray (who could eavesdrop on the dead, I think), watching everything.

The president was watching too, along with his ten-year-old son, Will, aka P.K., short for President's Kid. Aside from them, no one else in the government knew the president's daughter had been kidnapped. No one knew that the government had been infiltrated by terrorists either. As commander in chief, his job was to protect and defend the United States. As a father, his duty was to protect and defend his daughter. These two duties were now crashing into each other. He had called at least half a dozen times since we'd left the White House. I wondered what my father would have done if he was faced with the same situation . . .

The thought almost made me laugh out loud.

"Are you okay?" Angela asked.

"I'm fine." I had lengthened my pacing route from the bedroom way in the back to the snoring Croc in the passenger seat.

My bio father is Peter "Speed" Paulsen. He may be the best guitarist in the world, but he doesn't know what planet he's on half the time—make that three-quarters of the time. He has two full-time personal assistants to remind him to do things like eat and put on his pants. If I lived with him and got kidnapped by terrorists, it would take him a week to notice I was missing, if at all. I hadn't seen him since Mom married Roger, because of the restraining order. But I was sure he knew about the marriage. The whole world knew about the *Match* made in heaven. I was certain he wasn't happy about it, or their #1 hit.

He named me Quest after a hit song he wrote. It could have been worse. He had another hit song called "Zit." When I got old enough to know that Quest was a weird name, Mom suggested we get it legally changed. I passed. By then I was known as Q and I didn't mind the nickname except when my teachers spelled it CUE . . .

See what I mean by my busy mind? When I'm nervous, thoughts bounce around like bingo balls. Boone gave me a concerned look as I walked by for the tenth time, then looked at Angela.

"I think we'd better let him take his cards back out," he said.

Angela sighed. "Okay."

I pulled my deck back out and sat down and started to shuffle . . . quietly. Boone looked like he wanted to dive into the laptop screen and pluck Bethany from the backseat of the Tahoe. The strain of the past few days was etched into every wrinkle on his old face. It might have been my imagination, but his long gray braids and beard looked a shade lighter too. If this kept up, his hair might be snow-white by sunrise. His cell phone rang. He put it on speaker without picking it up from the table.

"Update," the president said without a hello.

"No change," Boone said. "Any intel from the interrogations?"

Malak and Angela had taken down two White House moles before Malak had snatched Bethany. Pat Callaghan and Charlie Norton, two Secret Service agents, had taken the moles to an undisclosed location and were *questioning* them, which probably meant something very different than the word implied.

"They've been sweated pretty hard," J.R. said. "They don't appear to know anything except their small part."

"Their part wasn't so small," Boone said, his eyes still on the laptop screen.

"Agreed," J.R. said. "The operation was perfectly compartmentalized. Arbuckle and Chef Cheesy didn't even know they were on the same team until this morning. I don't think they have any idea who gave them their instructions, or who else is involved."

"They were recruited somewhere by someone, and trained," Boone said.

"We'll get the whole story out of them eventually, but it won't help our current situation." The president paused for a long moment, then said, "I have a SEAL team on alert."

Boone turned away from the screen and looked down at the phone.

"What did you tell them?"

"I told them to stand by. No details." Another long pause. "I'm going to send them in, Boone. If I think it's necessary."

"Are you co-opting the operation?" Boone asked.

"Negative," J.R. answered. "But I'm tempted to. It's my daughter."

"I appreciate your restraint," Boone said. "This can't be easy. Are you still in the Oval Office?"

"No. I moved down to the Situation Room. P.K.'s still with me. The electronics and communications are better and more secure in here. We've locked ourselves in. It's driving the staff up the wall."

I could imagine. J.R.'s chief of staff, Mr. Todd, was a control freak. He had given Angela and me the third degree after our late-night meeting with the president in the Oval Office. We told Todd nothing about what was said, which nearly unhinged him.

"They called the V.P.," J.R. continued. "They told her that they thought I'd had a nervous breakdown. She rushed over here ready to take the oath of office. I told her that the rumors of my insanity were greatly exaggerated and sent her packing. But I'm not sure how long I'll be able to hold them off. Eventually I'll have to let them in on what's going on, or fire all of them for allowing terrorists to infiltrate the White House."

"You hired Chef Cheesy," Boone pointed out.

"Thanks for reminding me. When this is all over, I might have to fire myself too. But as we discussed, I'd like to take the ghost cell with me."

"We're doing our best."

"I know you are, Boone. I have complete confidence in you, but I've recruited some extra help."

Boone's blue eyes narrowed. "Who?"

"John Masters. You know him, right?"

"Our paths have crossed," Boone said quietly.

"Indonesia," J.R. said. "The hostage rescue during the volcanic eruption."

"I remember. I thought John hung it up after that. Settled down. Got married."

"He did. His wife died in an auto accident a couple years ago. He's been bumming around the country doing construction. He's living outside Tampa. We did a big favor for him in Mexico."

"What kind of favor?"

"We rescued him and his son . . . and a circus. Off the books."

"I imagine," Boone said dryly.

"What's important is that he's on his way to meet you right now. I scrambled a navy jet. They're in the air. Tampa to Norfolk. They should be landing soon. I was going to have him choppered up to meet you, but the hurricane makes that unlikely."

"What hurricane?" Boone asked.

Rain was pelting the windows and the wind was buffeting the coach, but it didn't seem that bad.

"You're driving into it," J.R. said. "Hurricane Jack. It just got upgraded from a tropical storm. They're predicting a landfall near Nags Head, North Carolina. Bad chopper weather. I'll put him in a vehicle and head him your way."

"He's been out of the game for a long time," Boone said.

"Not as long as you and your team."

"Our game is quite a bit different from John Masters'. We don't fight our way out of problems. We think our way out of problems. There's nothing the matter with our minds."

"You know as well as I do, Boone, that there are situations where thinking isn't enough. John wouldn't have come if he didn't think he was up to it."

"What did you tell him?"

"Everything," J.R. admitted. "I wasn't about to send him into this blind. I trust him. You can trust him. He has a Seamaster."

Boone glanced at me and Angela. "Good enough. I assume he's equipped with more than a hammer and screwdriver?"

J.R. gave a short laugh. "I have a full tactical kit waiting for him at Norfolk. He'll have plenty of tools, but no hammer and screwdriver. He'll check in with you when he lands."

"Fine," Boone said, but it was clear from his expression that he wasn't happy about the new addition to the SOS team.

"I'll keep you in the loop." He ended the call.

"Do you know this guy well?" I asked.

"Well enough. I worked with him a couple of times back in the day. He was the SEAL team expert in hostage rescue/recovery. Scuttlebutt was he had never lost a hostage. Don't know if the record held until he mustered out. And he has a Seamaster."

Angela and I glanced down at our watches. Having a Seamaster had nothing to do with the sea. The Seamaster was a Swiss watch made by Omega. The president had given us the watches the night before in the Oval Office. Boone had one and so did Angela's mom, Malak. Although she had taken out the tracking device, which J.R. used to keep tabs on his special friends. Engraved on the back of the case was the president's private phone number.

"How many of these watches has he given out?" Angela asked.

Boone smiled. "Don't worry. It's still a very small club." He hit X-Ray's speed dial. "Can you check out—"

"John Masters," X-Ray interrupted, which meant he had been monitoring Boone's cell phone. "I have him up on my screen. After he left the SEAL team, he moved to Portland, Oregon, and started a construction company with his wife's brother. They made a go of it for several years, then his wife and daughter were killed, then the economy tanked and the construction company almost went bust. About a year after that, he got struck by lightning and he and his son hit the road chasing storms, hiring out to fix the damage."

"Struck by lightning?" Angela blurted out.

"Yep," X-Ray confirmed. "Right in his backyard. He was in a coma for a week. But I guess he's okay now. I found a TV interview with him just before Hurricane Emily hit the Gulf coast of Florida this year. He was down there helping people get ready for the wind. The years have been kind to him. He looks pretty fit."

"What was he doing in Mexico?" Boone asked.

"The details are sketchy on that, but he was down there during the eruption of Mount Popocatépetl, and like J.R. said, there was a circus involved. A SEAL team flew down for an off-the-books extraction, which included the rescue of lions, tigers, and bears."

"Oh my," I added, completing the line from *The Wizard of Oz*, which got a laugh from Angela, a smile from Boone, and a compliment from X-Ray.

"Good one, Q," he said, and continued with his rundown on John Masters. "John and his son, Chase, came back to Florida, where John's been fixing hurricane damage."

"Until tonight," Boone said.

"Right. The president called him at twenty-two-oh-seven. They spoke for nineteen minutes. He was on an F-14 Tomcat twenty minutes after the call ended, heading to Norfolk Naval Station with an ETA of about five minutes."

"What about Hurricane Jack?" Boone asked.

"I'm tracking it. It's supposed to hit landfall at oh-two-hundred."

"Oh two hundred?" I asked.

"Military time," Miss Know-It-All said. "Two in the morning."

Spies can't even tell time normally.

"The wind is already picking up speed ahead of us," X-Ray continued. "Vanessa is having a hard time with the drone. If the wind gets worse, we're going to have to park it. I suggest we get a little closer to Malak."

"Got it!" Felix shouted from the driver's seat.

Apparently X-Ray had patched him into the conversation.

"No closer than a mile behind," Boone warned Felix, then turned back to the phone. "Keep the drone up for as long as you can." He ended the call and brought a weather map up on the screen. "When it rains it pours." A black swath of ugly clouds was blowing in from the Atlantic.

"Where are we in relation to the storm?" Angela asked.

Boone pointed to the screen. I could see we were just entering the northern edge of the ugly clouds.

"The only bright side is that the ghost cell wasn't expecting a hurricane either," Boone said.

"And we have a storm expert coming our way," I added.

"If he makes it." Boone traced his finger along John Masters' route. "He's going to be right in the thick of it."

In the Thick of It

John Masters thought he was going to crash and burn. The Tomcat bounced five times, like a winged basketball, before the pilot was able to get the jet to stick to the runway. The pilot pulled his helmet off and began to taxi. John pulled his helmet off too.

The pilot didn't look much older to John than his son Chase, which made John feel very, very old. He had called Chase just before he'd climbed into the cockpit in Tampa. It was a short conversation.

"I'm going to be out of pocket for a few days," John had said. "You won't be able to reach me."

"Where are you going?"

John was going to make something up, but he had promised Chase in Mexico he would always tell him the truth.

"I can't tell you any more than that. This cell phone isn't secure."

"I thought you were done with that stuff."

"Me too. But this guy I know has a . . . uh . . . family

problem and asked me to give him a hand. I owe him and couldn't refuse."

"Be careful, Dad," Chase had said, and asked no more questions.

John smiled as the pilot taxied toward a huge hanger. The guy was John Robert Culpepper, president of the United States. John had only met J.R. one time, many years earlier in Iraq, before J.R. became the president. John and his team had rescued an important asset in Iran without any fuss, meaning that they were in and out of Iran with no one knowing it and with the asset alive and well. J.R. had flown into Iraq for a personal debriefing. Highly unusual for the director of the Central Intelligence Agency. The debrief had lasted no more than fifteen minutes. At the end of it, J.R. took John into a room by himself and gave him a red box. Inside the box was an Omega Seamaster watch. John told him that he didn't wear a watch, that he always knew what time it was in his head almost to the second. J.R. took the watch out of the box and showed him the number engraved into the crystal on the back of the case.

"My personal number," he had said. "Someday you might need something from me. I'm ten digits away. Don't hesitate to call. I owe you."

John had put the watch away without ever putting it on his wrist, but not before memorizing the number. He had thought of that number many times over the years as he followed J.R.'s career. After John left the SEAL team and settled into private life, he didn't think he'd ever have a reason to use the number . . . until Popocatépetl. Desperate, John had stood on the ash-covered slope and punched in the number, not believing for a second that the president would actually answer. But he had. On the second ring.

"Culpepper. Who's this?"

"John Masters," he replied thinking the president would have no idea who he was. But again he was wrong.

"I hope you're not calling about the lousy economy and how it's affecting your construction business."

John was shocked. How did the president know he was in construction?

"No, sir," John said.

"Good. What can I do for you, John?"

Ten minutes later a SEAL team was scrambled to Mexico to rescue him, Chase, the Rossi Brothers' Circus, and dozens of injured villagers. After a few weeks helping to rebuild the village, he and Chase returned to Florida. Chase wanted to finish the school year in the same school. No more storm chasing. There was plenty of construction work after Hurricane Emily. John was as happy as he had been in years. Marco Rossi had given them a nice piece of property, and John was gathering material to build a home—a real home, a permanent home to take the place of the fifth wheel he'd been hauling behind his truck for two years.

Then the president had called. The conversation lasted less than half an hour. And it really wasn't a conversation. J.R. had done most of the talking. It was the most concise and organized mission briefing he had ever been through. What made it even more remarkable was that the president was talking about his own daughter's kidnapping.

Along with the rest of the world, John had watched the news coverage of the bombings in Washington, D.C. But he saw the attack through the calculating eyes of a former SEAL team member, knowing there was a lot more to the story than the media was able to dig up. They didn't know about the kidnapping, the ghost cell, the undercover agent posing as a terrorist, or the infiltration of terrorists into the U.S. government. The only people who knew were the president and a handful of ex-spooks led by the mysterious Tyrone Boone.

He had crossed paths with Boone twice, back in the day, without being certain who he was, or in what capacity he served the government. He had assumed the Willy Nelson look-alike was a CIA NOC agent–non-official cover–the most secret of the secret agents. John was surprised that Boone was in charge of the operation. In fact, he was surprised that Boone was still alive. The guy had been ancient twenty years ago. He had an image of Agent Hippy, as the SEAL teams had called him, tottering around a nursing home on an aluminum walker, pulling an oxygen tank behind him. But the president had been crystal clear. Boone was alive and well and completely in charge of the op. John was not to make a single move against the target without running it by Tyrone Boone first.

But first I have to find Boone, John thought as the Tomcat was hooked up and towed into the hanger.

A chopper was not waiting for him. Not surprising in this wind. The only ground personnel was the guy driving the tow truck. That wasn't surprising either. The fewer eyes on this the better. The ground guy pushed a set of the steps over to the cockpit. The pilot popped the cockpit hatch.

"Thanks for the lift," John said.

"No problem. Sorry about the bounce."

"We're on the ground in one piece. No foul." John climbed out of the cockpit. The pilot said nothing more. John knew the routine. The pilot had been ordered to pick up a civilian in Tampa and ferry him up to Norfolk without any questions.

John stretched the kinks out of his cramped muscles. At Mach 2 it had been a short flight, but the backseat of a Tomcat was a tight fit for his six foot two frame. There was a reason fighter pilots were called jet jockeys. Most of them were small. But they made up for their height with lightning quick reflexes.

Lightning.

John looked through the hanger door at the wind and the rain as a bright flash lit up the sky. He had been struck twice now, but lightning was the least of his problems. He started down the metal stairs and heard the pilot coming down behind him.

"No chopper tonight," the ground guy said as he reached the bottom.

"I figured," John said. "Kind of breezy out."

The ground guy nodded and pointed to a black SUV. "Keys are in the ignition. I was instructed to tell you that everything you need is inside. When you're ready to leave, take a right out of the hanger, then another right on Base Road. Security is expecting you. When they see the vehicle, they'll open the gate. No need to stop and ID yourself."

"Thanks."

The ground guy and the pilot climbed into a truck without

another word and drove out of the hanger, leaving him completely alone. He was in a hurry to get on the road, but he wasn't going anywhere until he checked every piece of equipment inside the SUV. The first thing he checked was the secure satellite phone. The unit was much smaller than it used to be—not much bigger than a cell phone. He turned it on and called Tyrone Boone.

Operation Medusa

"You're five miles behind," Boone said.

Felix eased off the gas. Wind gusts slammed into the coach, but he was managing to keep it under control. The same could not be said for the drone. The video of the Tahoe was bouncing all over the screen. Boone looked worried. His phone rang. He looked down at the number.

"I don't recognize it."

He let it ring until it stopped, then called X-Ray.

"I don't know the number," X-Ray said. "But it's an encrypted satellite phone."

"Must be John Masters' sat phone," Boone said. "He'll call . . ." *Incoming call* flashed across the small screen. He ended the call to X-Ray and answered. "Boone."

"John Masters."

"Welcome aboard. Where are you?"

"Norfolk."

"What's the weather like?"

"Lousy. Rain. Fifty mile an hour wind gusts. As soon as I

do an equipment check, I'll head your way. I'll be in a black SUV. Are you still on I-95 south?"

"Yeah. Does your SUV have an onboard computer?"

"Hang on." He came back on a few seconds later. "The computer's booting up."

"Can you link to it, X-Ray?" he said, getting him back on the line.

"Send out a ping," X-Ray said.

John laughed. "I would if I knew what you were talking about. You're going to have to walk me through this new technology. I've been unplugged for a long time."

X-Ray told him what to do and within a couple of seconds a video of John Masters fiddling with something on his dashboard appeared on our screen. With his blue eyes and chiseled features he looked like a Hollywood version of a Navy SEAL.

"Got it," John said. "Is that the target?"

"Affirmative," X-Ray answered.

"You're flying a drone in this weather?"

"So far," Boone said.

"Do you have a tracking device on the car?"

"After a fashion," Boone said. "Malak has one of our cell phones. Providing the battery holds its charge, or she doesn't dump it to keep it away from the bad guys, we'll be able to track her. The operative word is *her*. We have no way of knowing if Malak will be allowed to stick with Bethany, but my guess is she'll stick regardless of what the ghosts have planned."

"Someone knows the plan," John said.

"Maybe more than one," Boone said. "Malak thinks

there's an elite inner circle. Half a dozen people, maybe more. To take them down, we're going to have to cut off all the heads at the same time."

"Medusa," John said.

"Not a bad operational name," Boone said. "We're hoping the delivery of Bethany will transform Malak from a leopard into a snake head. Then we'll snatch Bethany back and make it look like it's not Malak's fault."

"Complicated," John said.

"It always is," Boone said.

"What about the battery on that cell phone she's carrying?" John asked.

Boone glanced at me. I looked at my Seamaster, trying to figure out the last time I had charged it. The cell phone Malak was carrying was mine. She had swiped it from the White House just before she snatched Bethany.

"It's been over thirty hours since I charged it," I said, feeling a little sick to my stomach.

"Did you copy that, John?" Boone asked.

"Unfortunately. What you're saying is that we're going to be operating unhooked by sunup or sooner."

"Looks that way."

"I'll be in touch," John said.

"Keep your comm set on. All of our cells are encrypted and can be linked. You'll know everything we know and you're welcome to chime in whenever you like."

"Is J.R. hooked into the phone tree?"

"Negative. And I know you're his guy, but I want to keep it that way."

John laughed. "I'm not his guy. I'm your guy by order of the president of the United States. Operation Medusa is all yours. You're in command. He made that crystal clear."

"Good to know," Boone said.

"See you down the road." John ended the call.

Boone's cell phone rang again.

"They're pulling over," X-Ray said.

Boone switched back to the drone stream.

"It's a rest area," X-Ray said.

The SUV pulled in next to three other SUVs.

"Uh-oh," Boone said.

"What?" Angela asked.

"The heat signatures." Boone pointed at the screen. "Four people in each car. Two in front. Two in back."

"They're all Chevy Tahoes," Vanessa chimed in. "I'm not sure how long I'll be able to keep the drone up."

"You have to keep it flying long enough for us to see what they're doing," Boone said calmly.

"They're getting out," Angela said.

The orange blobs were morphing into people as they climbed out of the SUVs.

"Punch it!" Boone said. "We need to get in front of them. Everyone needs to get in front of them."

The speedometer readout on-screen leapt from 70 MPH to 90 MPH in an instant. The laptop started to slide across the table. Angela caught it.

"I don't understand," she said.

I didn't understand either.

We stared at the screen.

"What do we have, X-Ray?" Boone asked.

"Sixteen people, but I can't say what gender they are."

"Can you sort them out?"

"Negative. There are trees in the way. I'll have to slow the video down and run it through a software program. That'll take at least an hour. Maybe longer."

"In an hour they could be seventy miles away heading in four different directions."

"Malak has my iPhone," I reminded them.

"But this is obviously a vehicle switch," X-Ray said. "There's no guarantee Bethany and Malak will stay in the same car."

The video started to go crazy.

"I'm losing the drone," Vanessa said. "It's going to crash."

"Land it," Boone said. "Preferably not on top of the terrorists."

"Not yet!" X-Ray cut in. "They're getting back in the cars. I need the vid of all the sequences or I won't be able to sort it out."

"Fine with me," Vanessa said. "It's not my million-dollar drone."

"Do your best," Boone said.

"We're passing the rest area," Felix called out.

Vanessa's best was about twelve minutes. We held our breaths as we watched them get back into the SUVs and turn back into orange blobs. One SUV backed out and started toward the exit followed several minutes later by a second, then a few minutes later a third, and then the drone crashed into what looked like a tree.

"Sorry," Vanessa said.

"You did your best," Boone said. "There's an interchange ten miles ahead with a truck stop. Everybody exit. We'll regroup there. X-Ray, keep tracking Q's phone."

"Got it," X-Ray said. "It's still at the rest area. Presumably with the last Tahoe."

The speedometer readout now read ninety-five miles an hour.

The Switch

Malak and Bethany had been yanked from the back of the car, thrown onto the ground, and covered with a large tarp.

"Stay perfectly still," someone said. "No talking."

Malak nearly laughed. There was no one to talk to. Bethany was still unconscious.

But she won't be for long on the cold wet ground with the wind and rain pelting this tarp, she thought.

The switch and scramble was a precaution against the Eye in the Sky. She doubted the SOS had a drone at their disposal, but the cell didn't know that. They were acting as if the full might of the U.S. government were after them, which was wise. They were taught to always proceed as if they were being watched. *You are a stranger in a strange land,* the manual of arms taught them. *You have no friends. Only enemies. And they are always watching.* The tarp was made out of a special material that cloaked heat signatures. Malak had laid under a cloak like this many times before in the deserts and mountains in far-off countries. She was pleased they had not tried to separate her from Bethany when they pulled them out of the Tahoe. If that had happened, the game would have been up. A lot of blood would have been spilled. She told the president that she would keep Bethany safe. She could not protect her if she wasn't with her.

So far so good.

She touched the pistol stuck in her waistband and hoped she wouldn't have to use it.

Yet.

She heard people shuffling aimlessly around the tarp.

Mixing themselves up. Confusing the Eye in the Sky. Little pieces being moved on a giant board.

Like the game "Simon Says."

Malak was not interested in the little pieces. She wanted Simon and his lieutenants.

It was difficult to hear above the wind and the rain, but after several minutes, it sounded like people were starting to move away. Carefully, she lifted the edge of the tarp. Car doors slammed, engines started. Malak pulled her pistol out and switched the safety off. If they were going to try to separate Bethany from her, it would be now. One of the Tahoes backed out, then a few minutes later another. She looked at her watch. Five minutes had passed. The third Tahoe backed out and drove away. Malak breathed a sigh of relief.

One left. They aren't going to separate us.

A gust of wind nearly blew the tarp off of them. Malak grabbed the edge and held it down. Bethany let out a moan and started to stir.

Not yet! Not now!

Bethany Culpepper tried to sit up.

The Itch

"Ziv and Eben. Cover the east exit. If a Tahoe comes by, follow it. Try to get a visual of the occupants, if you can. Uly, you cover the west exit . . ."

I looked out the window with longing as Boone snapped orders over his cell phone. There was a McDonald's at the truck stop. I didn't think I was hungry, but the golden arches got my stomach rumbling.

". . . X-Ray, keep working on those vids. We need to know which Tahoe they're in before we get too far away from each other."

"He's working on it," Vanessa said. "I don't think it's going well. He just plugged his noise cancellation headphones into his iPod Touch and turned the volume up to max."

"What about Q's cell signal?" Boone asked.

"I'm watching it while X-Ray tries to untangle the vid. The signal's weak. It's still at the rest area. Stationary. It hasn't moved an inch."

"That could be good or bad," Boone said to no one in

particular. "Let's brainstorm this thing. They could have taken it from her and dumped it . . ."

My brain was split between the conversation and the golden arches. . . .

Why are they called the golden arches? The arches are actually yellow. I guess yellow arches doesn't sound right, so they called them golden. But why didn't they just paint them golden? Probably because no one would see them. Gold doesn't stand out like yellow. I could look it up on my laptop. Why am I thinking about this anyway? It's not like I'm hungry. When I get nervous, the last thing I want to do is eat. There's something else going on. Something . . .

The itch.

Twice in twenty-four hours, which was a new record for me. The itch is kind of like a premonition, like absolutely knowing something is going to happen before it happens. The problem is that I never know what that something is going to be. This time it was more like a tickle than an itch, but it was definitely there, like a small spider crawling on my neck.

I tuned back into the brainstorming session. I'd missed some of the conversation. Ziv was talking. Of all of us, he knew Malak the best. "I'm the monkey that watches the Leopard's tail," he had told us. "I'm her second pair of eyes and ears. I make certain that no one stalks her while she stalks her prey." He had been covering Malak's tail since she became the Leopard. This included killing terrorists who suspected that his daughter was the Leopard.

". . . the phone perhaps," Ziv was saying. "But she would not leave the side of the daughter of your president."

Ziv wasn't from the U.S. I don't think anyone knew where

he was from.

"If they had found the phone, they would have smashed it," Vanessa said.

"Unless they want us to believe she's still there," Felix said. He had unbuckled and joined us in the kitchen. His crew cut cleared the ceiling by only about two inches. Croc sat next to him with his tongue hanging out because there weren't enough teeth in his mouth to hold it in. "There's only one way to find out."

"We have four directions to cover and only three vehicles," Vanessa pointed out.

"Truck stop is full of cars," Felix said.

Felix was big, but he was not a big talker. When he talked, it always sounded like each of his sentences took up a whole page—and he paused as he turned each page.

"Some of the cars belong to people working here," he said.

"They won't miss 'em 'til their shift ends," he added.

"Saw a nice Caddy parked in back when we drove in," he continued.

Boone grinned. "I don't know if the Cadillac is the best choice, but the idea is sound." He turned back to his cell. "Everybody got that? Felix is going to jack a car and head back to the rest area. If you see a Tahoe doubling back and heading north, let him know. He can pick it up and follow when it passes by."

Felix was out the door and heading across the parking lot before everyone had checked in. I watched him out the window. He bypassed the Caddy and stopped by a sports car he couldn't possibly fit into. He looked to his right and left, then did something with his big hands that I couldn't see. He opened the door and squeezed himself in. Five seconds later, the headlights came on and he drove out of the parking lot.

"First Tahoe," Vanessa said. "It's turning west."

Boone cursed. "You drive, Vanessa. Have Uly jump out and spot."

"No one to monitor Q's cell," Vanessa said. "X-Ray has his hands full. Their taillights are disappearing."

"Follow them, Uly," Boone said.

He looked at Angela and me. "One of you is going to have to spot."

"I'm faster," I said. "I'm better at sneaking around."

"I'm older," Angela said. "And I have a black belt in tae kwon do."

"Speed trumps age and we need to spot them, not kick them in the ears."

"Is your cell phone charged up?" Boone asked.

I knew he wasn't talking to me. I didn't have a cell phone. Angela pulled her phone out of her ratty backpack with a smirk.

"Eighty-five percent," she said.

"Give it to Q."

I'm not sure who was more surprised, me or Angela.

"Why?" Angela asked.

"Short answer, I promised your mother I would protect you."

I guess that meant I was expendable. But I didn't care. I wanted to do something. I needed to do something.

"And," Boone said, "someone has to monitor the computer. I'll be driving. You're more tech savvy than Q."

This seemed to satisfy Angela. She handed me her phone.

"You'll need to conceal yourself near the off-ramp, where you can see in all four directions," Boone said to me. "Croc will go with you. Hurry."

I wasn't sure how a toothless geriatric dog was going to help me spot terrorists, but I didn't stop to argue. I put on my coat and baseball cap and rushed out the door with Croc at my heels. I was nearly blown back into the kitchen by a gust of wind. Angela grabbed the laptop to protect it from the rain.

"You okay?" Boone asked mildly.

"Yeah. No problem. I can handle a little wind and rain." But this was a *lot* of wind and rain. Croc put his ears back, and waddled outside. I followed him, trying to hide my grimace as I struggled to close the door. I finally got it closed and looked around for Croc. He was christening the coach's rear tire.

"See you on the other side!" I said, and leaned into the wind. The truck stop was on the east side of the interstate. The off-ramp was on the west side. I had to get across the overpass before another Tahoe showed up. The wind was much worse over the interstate than it was at the truck stop. Halfway across, I glanced back at the coach. Croc was still frozen in place, staring at me with one brown eye and one creepy blue eye, like some obscene statue. I stuck earbuds in my ears so I could listen in on the spook phone fest. I had to turn the volume up to max to hear anything against the howling wind.

Felix was on his way to the rest area. The intellimobile was heading west behind Tahoe #1. Ziv and Eben were watching to the east.

I was about to report in when I saw a car driving up the off-ramp. It was too far away to see what kind of car it was, but it looked big enough to be a Tahoe. Its left-turn signal flashed. I hurried along, trying not to be too obvious, which was hard, because what was a kid doing walking across an overpass in the middle of the night, in the middle of nowhere, in a wind storm? I bobbed my head like I was rocking out through the earbuds—a pitiful cover, but what else could I do? The car turned and I saw the gold Chevy emblem on the grill.

Gold.

Yellow.

The itch.

There was something teetering on the edge of one of my brain cells that I couldn't seem to tip into consciousness. Something that had to do with the Tahoes and the rest area switch, something . . .

Something bumped into my leg. Croc. Two seconds ago he was still answering the call of nature fifty yards away. He wasn't even panting. Impossible. I glanced back at the coach to make sure he didn't have a toothless twin and saw that Boone had fired up the coach. Diesel exhaust was burbling out of the twin mufflers in back. I turned and saw that the Chevy was just about even with us. It was a Tahoe! I tried to see through the windshield without being too obvious. There were two men in the front seat, but I couldn't see them clearly. I turned my head away and spoke into the mic.

"Second Tahoe on the overpass heading east."

I tried to get a peek into the backseat as they passed. It was no good.

"Too dark to see into the back," I said. "I'm not sure if they're in there or not."

"They are heading east," Ziv said.

"Follow them," Boone ordered. "Q?"

"I'm here."

"Is Croc with you?"

"Yeah. Right next to me." I didn't mention that I had no idea how he had gotten right next to me.

"Good. He'll sniff out the best spot to hide and watch."

"Are you kidding?"

"This isn't Croc's first rodeo. Just follow his lead."

Great, I thought. Not only am I expendable, but I'm being led by a dog.

Undercover

Malak wrapped her arms around Bethany Culpepper, held her down, and spoke to her.

"My name is Malak Turner. You have been drugged and kidnapped. You must be completely silent. You must trust me. I'm with the Secret Service."

It felt good to say that she was with the Secret Service, even though it wasn't exactly true.

Not anymore. Perhaps someday it will be true again. Perhaps someday this will all be over.

Bethany stopped struggling.

"Listen to me very carefully," Malak whispered. "We don't have much time."

She explained their situation as accurately and concisely as she could in the few moments they had. Bethany lay so still that Malak thought she had passed out again.

"Nod if you understood what I just told you," she whispered.

It was a great deal to absorb after coming out of a drug-induced sleep and finding yourself hooded, lying under a tarp on the wet ground with the woman who kidnapped you claiming to be a deep-cover Secret Service agent. But Bethany's head moved up and down as if she understood. Malak found herself smiling in amazement and admiration. She had known Bethany for many years. When J.R. was the vice president, Malak had been in charge of his protective detail. As a teenager, Bethany had been smart, sensible, and a lot of fun to be around. It looked like courage had been added to her long list of attributes.

When Bethany's mother had died, she had stepped into the First Lady, or First Daughter, position without a hitch. It was rumored that J.R. had consulted her on every major decision he had made over the past six years. She was not just his daughter. She was a valued advisor. It was easy to see why.

Bethany said something that Malak didn't catch. Malak leaned in closer and asked her to repeat herself.

"The hood," Bethany said quietly.

"It's meant to frighten and disorient you. Unnecessary, I know, since you're supposed to be unconscious, but you'll have to leave it on. They can't see you, which works to our advantage. We need them to think you're incapacitated for as long as we can. As soon as you're awake, they will gag and flex-cuff you. When they get a chance, they'll put you in front of a video camera for all the world to see. The point of this exercise is to show the world that the U.S. government, and specifically your father, is vulnerable."

"Yoga breath," Bethany whispered.

"What?"

"It's a breathing technique for relaxation. I've practiced yoga for years. A necessity if you want to stay sane in my father's world. I'm an expert in relaxing under difficult circumstances. Although this is going to be a challenge."

Malak smiled. *No doubt about it. This is J. R. Culpepper's daughter.*

She checked her watch, surprised to see that fifteen minutes had past since the third Tahoe had pulled out. She looked out from beneath the tarp. The fourth car was still there, its parking lights on, the engine running.

What are they waiting for?

Suddenly a pair of men's boots came into view. They were wet and muddy. The tops of the scuffed boots were covered by frayed jean cuffs. Cell members came in all shapes, sizes, and ages, but they were usually well groomed and well dressed. The scuffed boots and frayed jeans could belong to an innocent bystander, Malak figured, someone curious about the tarp and what lay beneath. If he lifted the edge to look, there was a good chance that the Tahoe doors would fly open and Scuffed Boots would die where he stood. Malak had faced this situation many times before. Sometimes she was able to intervene without risking exposure, other times she couldn't and had to let nature take its course. This could be one of those other times.

Collateral damage. An ugly phrase to rationalize senseless violent death.

Malak had to at least try to save Scuffed Boots. She slowly pulled her pistol from her waistband. If he lifted the tarp, she would jump up, knock him out, then fire a couple of rounds into the ground near him. With luck, Will and Abe, or whoever her escort was now, would think she had killed him. The report and muzzle flash should be enough to spur Will and Abe into action, to change the grand plan. She was tired of lying on the wet cold ground. If Scuffed Boots was lucky, they wouldn't check to see if he was dead. He'd wake up in a few hours with a cracked skull and a bad headache, thinking some wacko had attacked him in a rest area. If they *did* check him and saw that the Leopard had missed from point-blank range, she would kill them, and there would be two less terrorists in the world.

Then what? That's always the question.

She thumbed the safety off, visualizing exactly what she was going to do step-by-step, then held her breath, readying herself for the first move. But she didn't have to make that move. Scuffed Boots dropped something on the ground, kicked it under the tarp, and walked away.

She exhaled and looked at the Tahoe. Parking lights on, engine running, Will and Abe still inside with the doors closed. A small light came on a few feet away from her. Scuffed Boots had kicked a disposable cell phone under the tarp. She answered.

"It is time," a man said. His accent was Middle Eastern. Yemen she guessed. "You will be moving on now."

"Along with my friend," Malak said.

"Of course. We are just your drivers."

"I will need help moving her."

"She is still . . ." he hesitated. "Asleep?"

"She was given too much. She'll be asleep for a long time."

The lie was met with silence, which did not surprise her. Cell members were given very specific orders. They were to carry out the orders to the letter. Sudden changes to the plan always threw them off. Independent action was frowned upon, except by the few in the upper echelon of the organization. Malak was a member of the few. Scuffed Boots obviously was not. In all likelihood, he had not been told who he was transporting. He was simply told to pick them up, and that one of them had been drugged. The delay at the rest area may have been arranged to allow Bethany a chance to regain consciousness, or perhaps to set up assets farther down the road. The reason didn't matter. It was time for Malak to take control of the situation.

Scuffed Boots finally broke his silence. "Is she healthy?"

"She's fine," Malak said impatiently. "But she is cold and wet. We have been here too long. We need to move her. Now."

"We are to keep you covered in the event there are—"

"Ridiculous!" Malak cut him off. "Drones cannot fly in weather like this. If there was a drone on us, do you think they would leave us alone here? This rest area would be swarming with police and military. The longer we stay, the more dangerous it becomes. You approached us. How long before a passerby does the same thing? Or perhaps it will be a state policeman on patrol."

"I will make a call."

"You do whatever you like, but I'm getting up. Are you familiar with the name Anmar?"

"The Leopard," Scuffed Boots said quietly. "What does he have to do—"

"The Leopard is not a *he*," Malak said. "If you want to live through the night, you will help me. Make your call down the road. You are talking to the Leopard, and the Leopard is moving."

Southbound

Boone was right. This wasn't Croc's first rodeo. He led me to the perfect spot to watch for the remaining Tahoe. We stood next to an old oak tree, with no protection from the wind and the rain, but it had a great view of I-95, the off-ramp, and the truck stop across the way. Boone thought there was a good chance that one of the remaining Tahoes, or maybe both, would bypass the exit and continue south. Luckily, there wasn't much traffic this time of night and most of it was semi-trucks. I stood there shivering, watching eighteen-wheelers and cars zip past, thinking that Tahoes looked similar to a lot of other SUVs, and there was a good chance that I would either miss the vehicle or misidentify it. I told Boone about my concern.

"You might miss the Tahoe, but Croc won't," he said. "The only reason you have to be out in this mess is because he can't use a cell phone."

In addition to being expendable, I was now a dog's personal assistant. *Great.* I looked down at Croc. His head was flicking back and forth like he was watching a tennis match. When I looked up, I saw the third Tahoe coming up the ramp. Its left-turn signal was flashing. I could see there were two guys in the front seat. I ducked behind the oak, but they didn't even glance in my direction. As they turned, I tried to see into the backseat, but again it was too dark.

"The third Tahoe is coming your way. Two guys driving. Too dark to see into the back."

"Okay," Boone said.

I watched it drive across the overpass. It went right past the truck stop and the coach. Then the left-turn signal came on again.

"Felix?" Boone said.

"Yeah."

"How far are you from the rest area?"

"Five minutes. Car's a piece of junk. Should have jacked the Caddy."

"You're going to have company," Boone said. "The third Tahoe is heading back north."

"Hope I can keep up with it."

"Just do your bes–"

Vanessa cut in. "The cell signal is gone."

Boone didn't say anything for a couple of seconds. No one said anything. We all knew what this meant.

"Where was it when it went out?"

"Exact same coordinates. Either the battery gave out or someone disabled it where it was."

The battery going out wasn't my fault. I didn't know Malak was going to steal it, or that it was going to be our only means of tracking her. But I felt guilty anyway. If President Culpepper had been listening in, he'd be freaking out. We had just lost track of his daughter.

"How's X-Ray doing unscrambling that video?" Boone asked.

"He's going through it frame by frame," Vanessa said. "By the sour expression on his face, I'd say it's not going well."

"We're switching to a visual protocol," Boone said. "We need to I.D. the people in the backseats so we can eliminate some of the vehicles. We're spread way to thin. The Tahoes are going to have to stop for gas eventually. All of you make sure you're in a good position when they do. If Malak and Bethany aren't in the backseat, let the Tahoe go and head back this way."

"We may have another problem," Vanessa said. "I've been monitoring the storm and they're reporting widespread cell tower outages to the south and east, and the satellite signals and radios are also getting funky. Emergency service workers are having a hard time communicating."

"When it rains it pours," Boone said. "Are you getting this, John?"

John's crackly voice came over the line. "She's right. The sat signal is weak and there's no service on the cell. I've picked up enough of the conversation to piece together what's going on, but not all of it."

"Where are you?"

John told him, which meant nothing to me standing out in the wind and rain next to an oak tree. I had no idea where he was compared to where we were. In fact, I didn't know exactly where we were.

"Start angling south," Boone said. "I suspect Bethany's in the fourth Tahoe and they're going to continue down I-95. Looks like we'll be trailing them solo. We may need backup."

"See you down south," John said.

No one said anything for about ten seconds, then Boone came back on the line. "Everyone else," he said, "you all know what to do. Most of you were doing this type of work long before we had all the gizmos. If Malak and Bethany aren't in your Tahoe, turn around.

Felix checked in. "I'm at the rest area. I see a lot of semi-trucks. A few cars. No Tahoes. No one in the restrooms. Looks like people are waiting out the storm. I'm heading out to the interstate to catch the third Tahoe. Out."

A Hummer came up the ramp. I recognized it from the big ugly grill. It was the same color yellow as the golden arches across the interstate. As it turned left toward the truck stop, I felt the itch again. Stronger this time. I looked at the driver. He was alone. My knees nearly buckled. The guy driving looked exactly like my dad, Peter "Speed" Paulsen. Which was impossible. My dad owns several cars, but doesn't have a license. According to my mom, he never learned how to drive. If they wanted to go somewhere alone without an entourage or a driver, she had to drive. It was one of the many things that drove her nuts when they were married. They were virtually never alone together. There was always someone with them. When they got divorced, he hired a platoon of housekeepers, a twenty-four-hour chef, yard and pool people, personal assistants, and he always had a dozen houseguests taking advantage of him. One of the reasons he had to tour almost constantly was to pay for the people he needed around him. His most recent hit was a song called "Solitude." Mom said the song was good, but it sure wasn't composed from the heart or personal experience.

And yet here he was driving a Hummer by himself in the middle of nowhere. I told myself that it couldn't possibly be him. But what about the itch? I watched the Hummer drive across the overpass and turn into the truck stop.

Croc started barking. Startled into reality, I turned back to the interstate, expecting to see the fourth Tahoe. Instead, the rodeo dog was barking at a truck.

"That's an eighteen-wheeler, Super Dog. You could stick a dozen Tahoes inside the trailer. See that big red crab on the side of the trailer? It says The Maryland Fish Company, not The President's Daughter Is Inside."

Croc gave me a dirty look and continued barking until the truck disappeared into the night. I glanced back across the interstate and tried to spot the Hummer, but I didn't see it. Maybe it had moved on. Or maybe the guy had parked the Hummer where I couldn't see it and he was inside washing down a couple of cheeseburgers and a load of fries with a vanilla shake, which is something my dad would do.

My dad had terrible eating habits, which was another thing that had bugged my mother when they were married. He weighed 159 pounds when he was fifteen years old, and he still weighed 159 pounds at 40-something. It took her years to lose the weight she gained while she was married to him. He didn't like to eat alone and he spent the entire day eating. He chewed and swallowed calories every minute of every day, except when he was sleeping or performing, and he never gained an ounce. I hadn't spent much time with him one-on-one, but the few times I had, the food was good and plentiful.

I was beginning to think that I hadn't felt the itch after all. That maybe I was just hungry. Mom said that I had inherited my dad's metabolism and hyper-personality. That I was like a shrew, constantly eating so I'd have the energy to constantly move. There was some truth to that, I guess. And it was highly unlikely that the guy driving the Hummer was my dad. There were a lot of guys who looked like him. In fact, he was so famous that there were Speed Paulsen impersonators in Las Vegas. Dad got a kick out of showing up and watching their shows.

Croc started growling. I turned my attention back to car spotting. The interstate, pelted by rain, looked like an empty parking lot.

"There's nothing there," I said. "Or are you still ticked off about the crab truck mistake?"

Croc fixed his weird blue eye on me and barked. Two seconds later, a Tahoe zipped by with water spraying up behind it.

I hit Boone's speed dial.

"The fourth Tahoe! It's heading south!"

"I'll be there in a minute," Boone said calmly.

Croc stepped out from our hiding place next to the oak and sat down on the road's shoulder, as if he had heard and understood the brief exchange. I joined him, thinking the night was filled with impossibilities.

The coach pulled out of the truck stop and drove across the ramp, as if Boone were a retiree heading to Florida for the winter. I was ready to jump in as he drove past, but he eased over to the shoulder and came to a complete stop. I whipped the door open and jumped through. Croc joined me, but at a more leisurely pace, and hopped into the passenger seat next to Boone.

"They have a three-minute head start!" I said.

Boone turned around. "Four minutes," he said. "They are probably going seventy miles an hour. At eighty-five miles an hour, we'll catch up to them in ten to fifteen minutes." He put the coach into gear, and pulled onto the interstate.

I turned and looked at Angela. She was eating a cheeseburger.

"I thought you might be hungry," she said, but it sounded like . . . *eh faw yeh my be hung flea* . . . because her mouth was full.

A half a second later, my *mowf us fill too.*

After two cheeseburgers, a large order of fries, and a vanilla milk shake, I was somewhat full, but the itch was still there. Boone was up front, talking to the president, while he followed the Tahoe south. Angela was sitting across from me, staring at the laptop. She had only drunk half of her milk shake. I wanted to ask her if I could have the rest of it, thinking it might scratch the itch, but instead I said, "I think I saw my dad."

She looked at me. "What?"

"My dad. Peter 'Speed' Paulsen. Driving a yellow Hummer."

She gave me a doubtful look, but she didn't laugh, which I appreciated. "Where?"

"He took the exit to the truck stop."

"Probably someone who looks like him."

"Have you ever seen him?"

She typed something into the laptop, then turned it around. The screen was filled with thumbnail photos of Speed Paulsen. Not exactly the kind of family shots most people have hanging on their walls. Speed on stage. Speed punching a photographer. Speed skinny-dipping on a public beach. Speed leaving a rehab clinic. Speed looking out the back window of a police car.

"Everyone knows what your father looks like," Angela said.

Dear old Dad, I thought staring at the photos.

Angela swung the laptop back around so she could see the screen. She started typing again. "It's not like your dad has a private life," she said. "Any more than my dad or your mom has a private life." She stopped typing. "Here we go."

I scooted over so I could see the screen. The headline read: "Speed Back in Rehab." There was a photo of him getting out of the back of a stretch limo, looking wasted and irritated at the person snapping his photo. After all these years, you'd think he'd be used to the paparazzi. Not surprisingly, he was surrounded by personal assistants, bodyguards, and hangers-on. It looked like they were all going to get a few days off, because the article said he was going to be in the Alcatraz Rehab Center for a minimum of two weeks. Rehab Rock, or the ARC, as it was called, was a relatively new facility. The old prison had been completely redone and turned into a trendy drug and alcohol recovery center. He had been admitted four days ago. The article went on to say that it was thought that his relapse was caused by the recent marriage of Blaze Munoz to Roger Tucker, and Match's successful album and sold-out tour.

I was sure he wasn't happy for them, but I doubted that had caused the relapse. He'd had a relapse every year since I was born. The point was, the guy in the Hummer was not my dad, because my dad was drying out three thousand miles away at a former federal penitentiary in the middle of San Francisco Bay.

But that still didn't explain the itch.

"Maybe it will work for him this time around," Angela said kindly, not mentioning that I was wrong about the guy in the Hummer. There were times that I really liked having her for a sister.

Boone must have ended his update to the president, because he called back to us that we had just crossed into North Carolina.

Angela switched back to the GPS and sure enough Virginia was behind us. I looked at my watch. It was 1:35 in the morning.

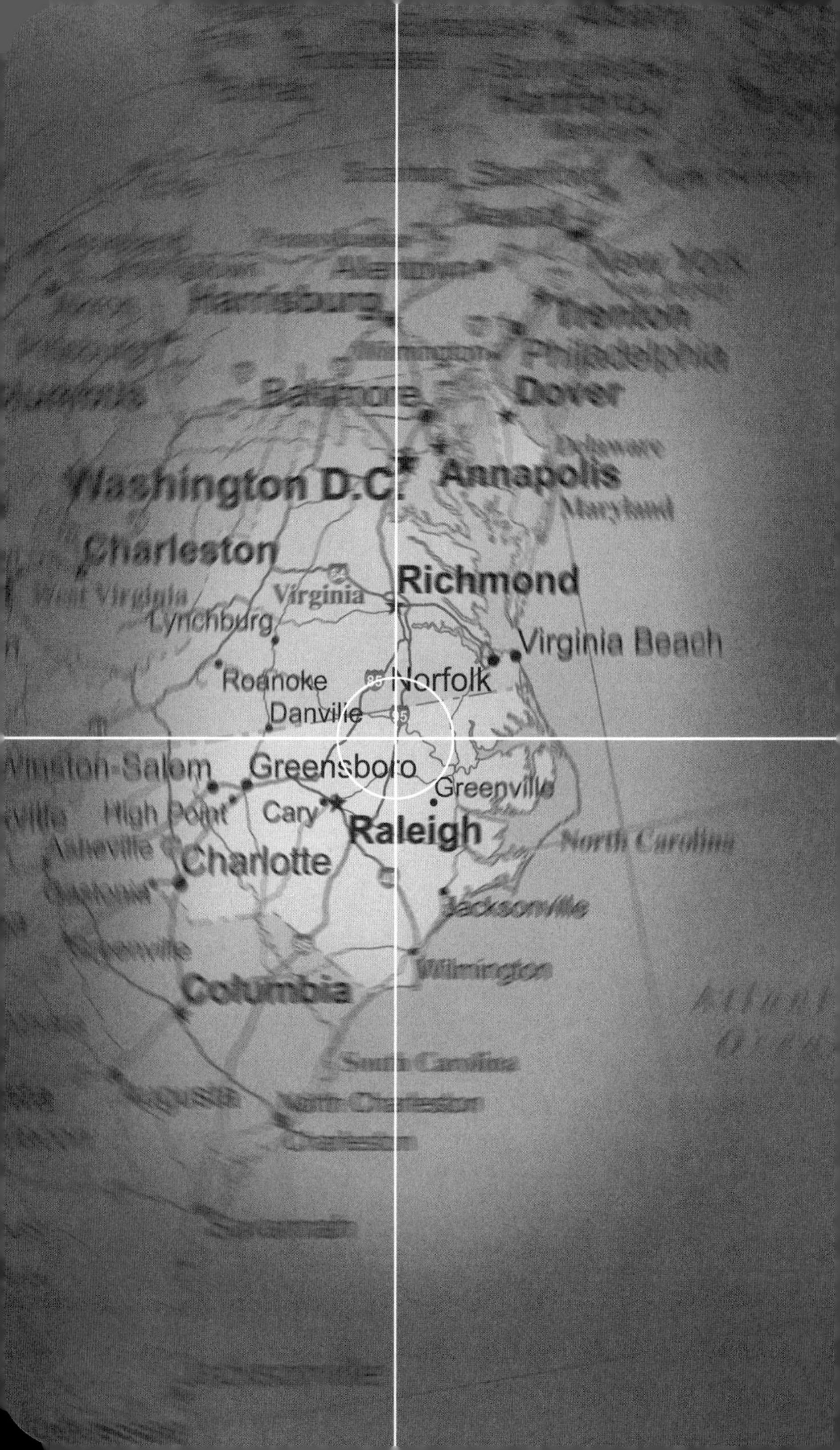
Harrisburg
Philadelphia
Baltimore
Dover
Delaware
Washington D.C.
Annapolis
Maryland
Charleston
Richmond
Virginia
West Virginia
Lynchburg
Virginia Beach
Roanoke
Norfolk
Danville
Winston-Salem
Greensboro
Greenville
High Point
Cary
Raleigh
North Carolina
Charlotte
Jacksonville
Wilmington
Columbia
South Carolina
North Charleston

SUNDAY, SEPTEMBER 7 >

1:35 a.m. to 2:36 a.m.

Northbound

Felix felt like he was driving a go-cart instead of a car. To see the road, he had to almost lie down flat in the narrow driver's seat. Whoever owned the car was a smoker. It reeked. The ashtray was overflowing with cigarette butts. He would rather sit next to Croc than an open ashtray, and wondered if stale smoke caused cancer.

Hope I don't die of the big C before figuring out who's in the Tahoe.

"If I can keep up with them," he muttered as he put the window down and tossed the butts out along with the ashtray. He left the window open, preferring the cold rain in his face to the rank stench.

To stay with the Tahoe, he had to go ninety miles an hour downhill to make up for what he lost going uphill.

He looked at the fuel gauge.

Quarter full. Or three-quarters empty. Or completely broken.

He tapped the gauge for the tenth time since stealing the car from the truck stop.

If you're going to steal a car, don't steal a junker. Grand theft auto is grand theft auto.

Another hill loomed before him. Steep and long. The Tahoe powered up like it was dead level. Felix jammed the pedal to the floor. The car wound up to a shuddering eighty miles an hour, then the speedometer needle started to drop.

75 . . . 72 . . . 69 . . .

The temperature needle edged up into the red.

67 . . .

The engine's gonna blow.

I did the guy that owns this piece of junk a favor.

Now he can go out and get a car that works.

63 . . . 59 . . .

He topped the hill going fifty-two miles an hour. When he came over the rise, he expected to see a pair of red taillights in the distance, traveling at a steady seventy miles an hour. He saw nothing but darkness.

65 . . . 71 . . . 79 . . .

He hit the first curve at eighty-two miles an hour and saw flashing hazard lights on the right-hand shoulder a half a mile ahead. He couldn't tell if it was the Tahoe or not. He eased up on the gas, trying to recall the other vehicles he had seen prior to the long hill. There had been two of them. A semi-truck and a BMW. He remembered the bimmer in particular, because it had breezed by him going about ninety miles an hour, and he wished he was driving it instead of this gutless wonder. The hazard lights weren't the right shape for the bimmer and it certainly wasn't a semi-truck on the shoulder. If he blew by them, he could pull off up ahead and catch them as they passed.

If they get the engine going.

Or the tire changed.

Or whatever the problem is.

The farther north they went, the more exits there were. If he got too far in front, they could take an exit behind him. And then there was the gas problem. Eventually, he was going to have to stop. If they got off I-95 while he was filling up, he'd never find them again. The flashing lights grew brighter. It was definitely the Tahoe. He tapped the brake.

If the president's daughter is in the backseat, would they really turn on the hazard lights?

Felix put his brights on and pulled in ten feet behind the SUV. He sat there for a moment. The occupants were still in the vehicle. Steam, or maybe smoke, was billowing out from under the hood. He figured it was steam, because who would stay in a car that was on fire. He pulled a pair of binoculars out of his kit and looked through the back window. They wouldn't be able to see him past the headlights. There were four people in the car. The two in the back were women. They had turned their heads and were looking at him. They were not the Leopard, or the president's daughter. He couldn't see the two people in the front clearly.

If he drove off now, they would probably call in the weird encounter to their handler. If he didn't get out in the next few seconds and ask them if they needed help, they would become more suspicious than they already were.

He tossed the binoculars on the passenger seat, checked his gun, then unfolded himself from the little car. He knew that the most dangerous part would be the approach. He would be backlit by the headlights and completely exposed. At six foot seven and nearly three hundred pounds, he was a big target. The trick was to walk up on them in a friendly matter as if he wasn't expecting to be shot, or intending to shoot them, which he was happy to do if that's how they wanted to play it.

When he got to the window, he squatted down so his belt buckle wouldn't be in the driver's face and to protect himself behind the door. He wrapped his hand around his gun as the window slowly slid down.

Felix tried to put a sympathetic smile on his face. "Car trouble?"

The man returned the smile. He was in his mid-thirties, clean shaven, dark hair, light eyes, good teeth.

"I'll say," he said, nodding toward the steaming hood. "I think it's the radiator."

American accent. He didn't look or sound like a terrorist, which Felix supposed was the whole point. He looked at the man sitting next to him. He looked as clean-cut and normal as the driver.

"Did you call a tow truck?" Felix asked.

"It just happened," the man said. "We're still debating what to do."

Felix glanced at the women in the backseat. They both smiled at him as if they didn't have a care in the world. This bothered him. Being stranded on a rainy interstate in the middle of the night is upsetting. They looked like they were at a major intersection in a big city, waiting for a red light to turn green. All four of them had flashing Bluetooths in their ears, making them look like a group of terrorist cyborgs. He was also bothered by the fact that he couldn't see any of their hands. The driver was twisted around and leaning forward in such a way that Felix couldn't see his or the passenger's lap.

"I could take a look," Felix said.

"Are you a mechanic?"

"I know my way around engines. Pop the hood."

The driver had some trouble figuring out where the hood release was.

Not his wheels.

Throwaway car.

Felix moved to the front of the Tahoe and opened the hood. No one got out to give him a hand, or to see what he was doing. It was raining and the wind was blowing, but you would think one of them would brave the elements to join the Good Samaritan trying to help them out.

When the SUV broke down, why didn't they take a look at the engine and try to help themselves?

The answer brought a grim smile to his face. They were told not to. A breakdown was not on their agenda, nor was a stranger showing up to help them.

They're waiting for further instructions, or for someone else to help them, which explains the flashing hazard lights.

Four against one is okay.

Four-plus against one could be a problem.

He took the flashlight out of his left coat pocket, keeping his right hand on the pistol in his other one. A radiator hose had come loose. A simple fix with a pair of pliers. He had his multi-tool clipped to his belt, but he didn't reach for it. He wasn't sure he wanted to fix their car. He looked at the battery.

There were three wires hooked to it that didn't belong there. A red wire, a blue wire, and a green wire.

Uh-oh.

The wires explained why they had been told to stay in the car. There was a good chance they didn't know what the wires were or what they led to. But Felix knew, and he was beginning to think that stopping wasn't one of his better ideas.

X-Ray had given him a Bluetooth earpiece, but he had tossed it on the passenger seat. It hurt his ear and he thought flashing earpieces looked stupid.

Who's stupid now?

He needed to call Boone and tell him the good news and the bad news. The good news was that the targets weren't in this Tahoe. The bad news was the Tahoe was carrying more than passengers.

Taking a cell out in front of them and making a call would be just as threatening as pulling his gun and firing a round through the windshield. He'd have to make the call without them seeing, and he'd have to make it quick. He put the flashlight down and reached for his phone, then he heard a car door open.

Too late.

He picked the flashlight back up.

Time to play big dumb slow guy.

It was a role he'd played many times before, to great effect. The only part of the equation that was true was the big part. Three more doors opened.

Looks like their handler called and told them to get rid of the Good Samaritan.

He wondered if the handler had mentioned the three wires. He hooked his finger under the green wire and looked to his left. There was a steep slope on the other side of the guardrail.

Two running steps and a dive.

The driver came around the front with a big smile and a gun laid flat against his leg.

Big dumb Felix glanced at him, acting like he hadn't seen the gun.

"It's just a radiator hose," Felix said.

"If you got a pair of pliers I can hook it back up," Felix added. "I'll have you on your way in a jiffy."

"We don't have any tools."

This came from the guy who had been sitting in the passenger seat. He had walked up on Felix's left. One of the women was standing behind him. They weren't smiling now.

Felix looked back at the driver. The second woman had joined him. She wasn't smiling either. He wondered if their handler was listening through their Bluetooths. He hoped so, because he was about to get an earful.

"I have pliers in my rig," big dumb Felix said. "I'll grab them. Y'all should just get back in your car. No use in all of us getting drenched. You'll have to top off your radiator with water at the next gas station. That should get you where you want to go. I don't see any other problems. I'll grab my toolbox."

"You're not grabbing anything," the driver said, and raised his pistol.

Big dumb Felix feigned shock and fear. "Hey! Is that a

gun?"

He put his left hand up in the air, making certain the flashlight was shining in the eyes of the two behind him, temporarily blinding them. He stepped back one step.

"Wrong place, wrong time," the driver said.

Felix snapped the green wire, took two running steps, and dove over the guardrail. The blast pushed him thirty feet down the embankment. He tucked and tried to roll, but the roll turned into a thud. He landed flat on his back at the bottom of the slope, with every ounce of air driven from his lungs.

He lay with his mouth open and his eyes bulging, watching fiery debris falling all around him. He couldn't seem to move and wondered if his back was broken. He couldn't breathe and wondered if the impact had burst his lungs. A smoking bucket seat landed five feet from where he was lying. It didn't make a sound as it struck and bounced away into the darkness. He added deafness to his list of major problems.

He lay there for what seemed like an eternity, but was probably no more than a minute, waiting for that first breath. It finally came in the form of a gigantic gasp. He was going to wait a few moments before checking to see if his back was broken, but he hurried the schedule along when he realized that his coat was on fire. He was on his feet in an instant, tearing the coat off and stamping the fire out. It seemed that his back was not broken. The only things that didn't seem to be working were his ears. He couldn't hear a thing. He *felt* a crunch under his foot and swore, although he didn't hear the actual word.

He reached into the pocket of his smoking coat and pulled out what was left of his cell phone. He tossed the smashed plastic on the ground. He pulled his gun out of the other pocket. It was a bit charred and scuffed, but it looked serviceable. He stuck it in his belt. He had no idea where his flashlight had gone, but he didn't need it. Several trees had caught fire and were lighting the ruined landscape like torches. He started back up the slope. Nothing was broken, but every square inch of his body hurt.

It took him a lot longer to get to the top than it had to get to the bottom. He knew the explosion had been big, but that didn't prepare him for the damage to the interstate. The Tahoe and the sports car were gone, along with the four terrorists, the shoulder where they were parked, and a good portion of the inside lane of I-95 North. Blast debris was scattered across all four lanes, some of it still burning, but the heavy rain was dousing the fires. He looked up and down the road. No one had come along yet, but he knew when they did and reported it, this section of I-95 would be swarming with police. He didn't have time to talk to the police. And what could he tell them? Not the truth. That was for sure. He needed to get to a phone and tell Boone and the others the Tahoes weren't just there to confuse them. They were there to kill and cause chaos.

There was an exit two miles ahead. He started jogging north, ignoring the pain, wishing he could hear his footsteps.

Eastbound

"We are getting farther away from the Leopard," Ziv said. "I can feel it."

He was in the passenger seat. Eben Lavi was leaning over the steering wheel, trying to see past the furious wiper blades sluicing rain off the Range Rover's windshield. Boone had just called in and told them he was following the fourth Tahoe south on I-95. They were a hundred yards behind the second Tahoe, traveling exactly seventy-four miles per hour.

"What do you mean you can feel it?" Eben asked.

"I have been protecting Anmar for so long, I simply know when I am far from her," Ziv answered.

Eben didn't disagree with the old man. He thought they were following the wrong car as well. It was obvious that the purpose of the Tahoes was to divide them, and they were playing their part perfectly.

"How convinced are you?" he asked.

"Ninety percent."

"Are you thinking about a confrontation to speed things along?"

"That is exactly what I am thinking."

"It could be dangerous. If we are wrong and Malak and the daughter are in the backseat, the mission is blown."

"If Malak is in the backseat, we will not be alive to care. She will shoot both of us for ruining the Medusa operation, as Tyrone Boone is now calling it."

"And if she isn't there, and they make a call to tell their handler about the confrontation?"

Ziv reached into the bag at his feet and pulled out a magnetic police light and portable siren. "They will tell the handler that they have been pulled over on a routine traffic stop." He pointed at the speedometer. "They are exceeding the legal speed limit by four miles an hour."

"That hardly warrants a traffic stop. And we have no uniforms."

Ziv tossed a wallet into his lap. Inside was a police badge.

"You will have to be a plainclothes state trooper if they ask, which I doubt they will," he said. "You will be on the right-hand side. They will not be able to see past your flashlight. Look at the westbound traffic. We will ask them why they are in such a hurry to get to a hurricane. Very suspicious behavior."

The westbound traffic was a lot heavier than the eastbound traffic. In fact, aside from the Tahoe, they hadn't seen another vehicle heading in their direction in the past ten minutes.

"I don't think they will believe that."

"Their left taillight is out."

"No it isn't."

"It will be."

"What about Tyrone Boone?" Eben asked.

"He instructed us to get a visual on them. We are carrying out his orders. We are getting low on fuel. I suspect that they filled up before they arrived at the rest area. We will have to stop for gas before they do. If that happens, there is a good chance that we will lose them."

Eben nodded. "What else do you have in that bag of yours?"

"I have everything we need." Ziv started to unbutton his shirt. "Including a police uniform. Never leave home without one."

Westbound

Vanessa turned around in the passenger seat and looked back at X-Ray. His thick black glasses were askew, his white hair was sticking straight up from running his hands through it, his face looked like death in the light of the computer monitor. She knew better than to ask him how it was going, and it was obvious how it was going by the stricken look on his face. She had seen the look before, but not often.

"Epic failure," she whispered.

Uly looked over at her. "Huh?"

"Never mind," she said, wishing they could pull over so she could drive. Uly's neck had to be bothering him. He was so tall he had to put his chin on his neck to see through the windshield. She glanced at the speedometer. They were seventy-two miles west of I-95 and probably well over a hundred miles from Boone by now, and even farther from Ziv, Eben, and Felix. The Tahoe's taillights were a couple of hundred yards in front of them. It had stayed within the speed limit and in the right lane except to pass trucks and slower cars. If Bethany and Malak were not in the backseat, Vanessa wondered what instructions the occupants had received. Drive west until you run out of gas, or until you are pulled over and arrested, whichever comes first? Did they know each other? What were they talking about? How were they receiving their instructions? Cell phones? What was the endgame?

She turned around to look at X-Ray again, expecting to see their surveillance genius arguing with his computer, but he wasn't. He had straightened his glasses and had flattened his white hair. He was staring at her through his thick lenses.

"It's no good," he said. "There were two many trees, too much distortion in the stream. I have no idea what happened after they got out of the Tahoes. Dead end. We need to get a look inside that car."

"How?"

"We can do a drive-by with concealed cameras, but it will have to be timed absolutely perfectly. We'll have to pass them as they are passing under lights. The more services at the exit, the more lights. Our first shot is about ten miles ahead, but we'll have to come up on them easy so we don't spook them."

"Pull over," Vanessa said. "I'll drive."

Uly pulled onto the shoulder. They changed places and were back on the highway within seconds. Vanessa gunned the van until they saw the Tahoe's taillights again, then eased off the pedal. She glanced over at Uly. He was cracking his neck and seemed happy to be riding shotgun. She looked in the rearview mirror. X-Ray was scrambling around in the back, assembling equipment.

"You ready?" she asked.

"Not yet," X-Ray said. "But I will be by the time you make the pass. It's kind of old technology. I should have thought of it before, instead of screwing around with that drone stream for so long. We'd be way ahead of the game right now."

"It's not your fault," Vanessa said.

"Yes it is," X-Ray insisted. "I'm the one that asked Boone to get the drone. Sometimes the old way is best. We should have spent our time putting tracking devices on those vehicles, but no, I wanted to try a drone out. Stupid!"

X-Ray was far from stupid, and it was Vanessa who had flown and crashed the drone, but she let him *drone* on. She had known Raymond Brock for nearly fifty years and had worked with him all over the world. She had seen this self-recrimination bit several times before and knew he needed to get the mistakes of the past few hours out of his system before he could focus his formidable intellect on the problem at hand.

"Stupid!" he repeated.

Then it was over. Just like that. He took a deep breath and gave her a smile. "You better keep your eyes on the road or you'll crash the van too."

She returned his smile in the rearview mirror. "You just snap your photos and let me worry about the driving."

"Not photos. Video. I set up two cameras on the right side. I can control them with the computer, but they're nothing special, cheapos. You'll have to pass them slowly, but fast enough so they don't get suspicious. After we get the video, we'll be in front of them, which is a problem. They're not likely to forget this van. It will be hard to get behind again without them noticing."

Vanessa was well aware of how difficult it was to tail someone with one vehicle. Especially a vehicle that was looking for a tail. To do it right, you needed a minimum of three vehicles. Five or six would have been better. One vehicle was bad. One that looked like the intellimobile was very bad.

"Leave that to me," she said with more confidence than she felt. What she hoped was that the video would prove Bethany and Malak weren't in the car and she could hang a U-turn and rush back to I-95. She looked over at Uly. "Don't look at them as we drive by. You'll scare them. Act like you're asleep."

"I will be asleep," Uly said.

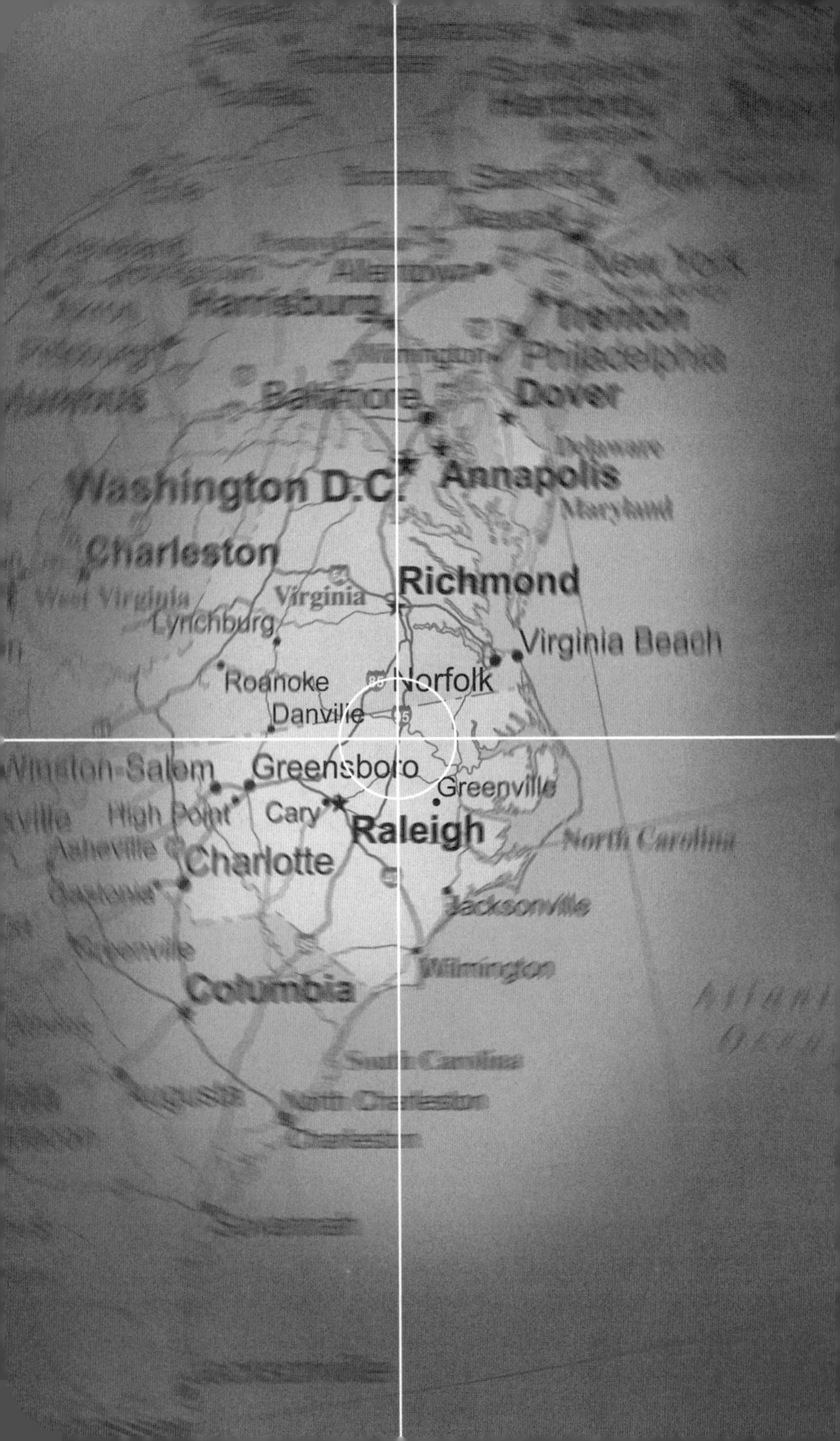

SUNDAY, SEPTEMBER 7 >

2:36 a.m. to 4:00 a.m.

Walk Away

I got a little bored watching the GPS and satellite images of Hurricane Jack, which we seemed to be driving right into, so I kicked Croc out of the passenger seat and joined Boone up front. Croc jumped up on the sofa and gave me the one-blue-eye glare before curling up and going back to sleep.

There were a pair of taillights about three hundred yards in front of us, which I assumed belonged to the Tahoe. The trees along the road were whipping back and forth as fast as the wiper blades. Boone had both hands on the steering wheel.

"You okay?" he asked calmly as if controlling the coach in this wind was the easiest thing he'd ever done.

"I guess," I said. "I mean, I'm tired and a little nervous and . . ." I didn't want to tell him about the itch. I'd never told anyone about the itch. How do you tell someone about something that you don't understand yourself?

Boone glanced at me. "And?"

I stared at the distant taillights, debating whether I should tell him or not, when a call came in. He tapped his earpiece to take it, then immediately tore the Bluetooth out of his ear and nearly lost control of the coach.

"What happened?" Angela shouted.

I turned around. She was at the kitchen table, clutching the laptop. Croc was getting up from the floor, glaring at the back of Boone's head as if he had dumped him from the sofa intentionally. Boone stabbed a button on the steering wheel and we caught Felix over the speaker in mid-sentence . . .

". . . caught fire. Stepped on my cell."

He was yelling, which is probably why Boone had yanked the Bluetooth out of his ear.

"You're shouting," Boone said in a normal voice. "We can't understand you."

This was followed by a pause long enough for Angela to join us up front. She squatted between us with the laptop. "His cell phone is offline," Angela said quietly. "I wasn't keeping track of the phones. Sorry."

"No worries," Boone said, then turned his attention back to Felix. "Are you there?"

Felix responded using one sentence per page.

"Yeah."

"Barely hear you."

"Explosion messed up ears."

"Explosion?" Boone asked.

"I'll start from the beginning."

Even from the beginning, it was a little hard to follow. The good news was that Malak and Bethany weren't in the Tahoe. The bad news was that the Tahoe had blown up along with the four terrorists and part of I-95.

"Found red, blue, green wires on the battery."

"Pulled green."

"Boom."

Felix was calling from a pay phone at a Cracker Barrel restaurant a couple of miles north of the explosion. The blast had blown out his eardrums and he had caught on fire. He wrecked his phone stamping his jacket out. He said his hearing was coming back. He was going to steal another car and head south.

"Take me a while."

"Sirens going by."

"I-95 will close."

"Have to go around."

He was talking loudly, but he wasn't shouting anymore.

"What about exposure?" Boone asked.

"We're good."

"I think."

"They thought I was a country bumpkin trying to help them."

"When they told their handler I was under the hood, they were told to take me out."

"I guess."

"Ghosts didn't know they were driving a bomb."

"Wouldn't have let me under the hood if they had."

"Mistake."

A mistake for them, I thought. Boom.

"Vanessa? Ziv?" Boone said. "Are you picking this up?"

We waited for a response. There wasn't one.

"Keep me posted, Felix," Boone said. "Try to get your hands on another cell."

At two-thirty in the morning he meant steal someone's cell phone. I doubted the Cracker Barrel sold them.

Boone looked at Angela. "Get on your phone and try to get in touch with Vanessa and Ziv. Keep calling until they answer. Tell them what's going on."

"What *is* going on?" Angela asked.

I wasn't exactly sure what was going on either. Felix had been shouting in a shorthand that only Boone seemed to understand.

"The terrorists are bundling the mission," Boone said. "Or at least the people running them are bundling. The Tahoes aren't just there to throw us off track. They're bombs. Probably all four rigs are, including the one hauling Bethany and Malak. The wires Felix saw led to a remote trigger and a tracking device. We're not the only ones watching the Tahoes. They're on their way to targets. He'll probably blow them at the exact same moment, pulling law enforcement away from whatever he plans to do with Bethany, unless we can defuse them first."

"We have to stop them," Angela said.

Boone shook his head. "That's the last thing we want to do. Felix got away with it because they broke down before he showed up. If we take out another Tahoe, whoever's running this dance will be onto us. Ghost cell operatives aren't suicide bombers. They're going to park the Tahoes and walk away. We need to follow them to their parking places and disarm the bombs after they walk away."

Apparently I was going to add defusing car bombs to my spy repertoire.

Smoke and Mirrors

Officer Ziv flashed the police light and gave the Tahoe a blast of the siren. The driver didn't hesitate. The Tahoe immediately slowed down, eased onto the shoulder, and came to a stop.

"Malak and Bethany are not inside," Ziv said. "If the president's daughter was in the backseat, the driver would have at least hesitated."

Eben nodded in agreement.

"We will make this quick," Ziv said. "I will take the driver's side, ask them a couple of questions, then let them go."

Letting terrorists go was not something Ziv was used to, but in this case it was the right call. If they killed them, the mission would be blown. They got out of the Rover into the wind and the rain, which seemed to be letting up a little. Ziv walked up on the driver's side. Eben took the passenger side. Both men held flashlights in their left hands. Eben had his gun in his right hand, held close to his body so they couldn't see it beyond the flashlight beam.

Ziv matched Eben's movement step for step, shining the

bright light into the windows as he approached. There was a man and woman in the backseat, another man and woman in the front. The women were clearly not Malak and Bethany. As he passed the rear end of the Tahoe, he made a swift movement with the ice pick in his hand, and the left taillight blinked out.

The driver's window slid down as Ziv walked up to it. He put the ice pick in his pocket so his right hand would be free for his gun. A woman was behind the wheel.

"Is there a problem officer?" she asked with a pleasant smile.

Ziv returned the smile and answered with his best southern accent. "May I see your driver's license and vehicle registration, ma'am?"

As she fished in her purse, he shined his light on the three passengers. They were all in their early to mid-thirties. They were completely relaxed. They smiled. Not a shifty eye among them. He would not have guessed in a million years that any of them were terrorists. It was disturbing. Now that he knew that Malak and Bethany were not inside, he wanted to leave, but if he didn't make the stop look legitimate they would become suspicious.

The woman handed him her license and registration. Her name was Alex Finn, she was thirty-two years old, and resided in Bethesda, Maryland. It could be her real name and real address, or it could be fake. At this point it didn't matter.

"I wasn't speeding," Alex said.

"You were a little over the speed limit, ma'am," Ziv said. "But that isn't why I pulled you over. Your left taillight is out."

"It is?" Alex seemed surprised.

Ziv nodded. "Bad night to have a taillight out. Low visibility. Could cause an accident. Do you know that you're heading into a hurricane?"

"Yes," Alex said. "We've been listening to the reports on the radio. We have a meeting tomorrow in Norfolk. We work for an architectural firm in Virginia."

That information jibed with the vehicle registration. The Tahoe belonged to an architectural firm.

"I doubt your meeting is going to happen tomorrow," Ziv said. "Norfolk is getting battered."

"We were just talking about that," Alex said easily. "It's too late to turn back. We were talking about checking into a hotel up ahead until morning."

"That's a good plan," Ziv said. "Before you head out tomorrow, get that taillight looked at. It's probably just the bulb."

Alex gave him a bright smile. "No ticket?"

Ziv thought about shooting her where she sat, but instead he returned her smile and tipped his hat. "Not tonight, ma'am," he said. "Drive safe."

◇ ◇ ◇

As Ziv was telling his carload of terrorists to drive safely, Vanessa was driving past her carload of terrorists. She had timed the pass perfectly, starting it just as the Tahoe reached the brightly lit exit area. She drove by slowly but steadily, careful to keep her eyes on the road without a glance to her right. True to his word, Uly was slumped in the passenger seat sound asleep. As she went by, her cell phone rang, but she ignored it, not wanting anything to interfere with her concentration. When she got by the Tahoe, she increased her speed slightly to give them the impression that she had been going faster during the pass than she actually was. She eased back into the right-hand lane fifty yards ahead, where she could keep track of them in her side-view mirrors. She felt herself smiling with satisfaction. It had been decades since she'd had to make a move like this.

Tracking devices take half the skill and all of the fun out of tailing someone, she thought. *How do you tail someone when you're in front of them?* She glanced at the Tahoe's headlights and her smile broadened as she answered the riddle. *With smoke and mirrors.*

If it turned out that Bethany and Malak were in the Tahoe, she had two ways to get back behind the vehicle. She could take an exit with an immediate on-ramp and drop in behind them after they passed. Or she could very subtly slow the intellimobile over several miles, letting them creep up on her until they couldn't stand it anymore and blew by her. She preferred the latter method to the former, because it would be their choice, and therefore they would be less suspicious about the old van behind them. Her tailing strategy was interrupted by X-Ray.

"Got 'em," he said. "All four of them turned to watch us pass."

"Bethany and Malak?"

"Not even close. Four kids. Two girls. Two boys. Twenty-year-olds, maybe younger. I'll run facial recognition on them and see if something pops, but you can definitely turn this rig around and floor it back east. The targets aren't in this Tahoe. I just wish I'd thought of this sooner. We could have eliminated them a hundred miles ago."

Vanessa glanced at the GPS. The next exit was a little over three miles ahead. Her cell rang again. This time she answered.

"Thank God!" Angela said.

Pass

"I have Vanessa!" Angela shouted.

She had been trying to reach the other two teams for ten minutes and we were beginning to think something bad had happened to them.

"Ziv and Eben are calling in too," Angela said.

"Put them all on speaker," Boone said.

"The footage from the rest stop was a bust," Vanessa said. "But we just did a drive-by and got some vid. The Tahoe had four kids in it, looking like they're out for a joyride."

"It is the same here," Ziv said. "We had a good look at them. They were older than Vanessa's group, but they are definitely not the people we are looking for. We are heading back your way."

"You need to turn around and reacquire them," Boone said. "Right now. Are you still in pursuit, Vanessa?"

"After a fashion. They're following us, but I can change that. What's going on?"

Boone told them about Felix and the bomb. Halfway

through his briefing, there was the screech of tires and what sounded like a car accelerating. I figured it was Eben turning around and making up for lost time.

When Boone finished, Ziv said, "We will catch up to them and take them out."

"Negative," Boone said. "I want you to follow them. No confrontation. No interference."

"Is Felix okay?" Vanessa asked.

"A little singed, a little deaf," Boone answered. "I think he managed to get rid of the terrorists cleanly. Accidents happen when you're hauling a bomb around, but we won't get away with it again. The ghosts aren't suicide bombers. Their motto is 'live to kill again.' I think the other two will park their rigs near high-value targets and walk away. That should give you some time to disarm the bombs before they go off. Is that clear, Ziv? Eben?"

Both men said yes, but they weren't enthusiastic yeses.

X-ray chimed in. "They'll know we're onto them when the bombs don't explode."

"Hopefully by then, this will all be over," Boone said. "I doubt they're going to detonate the bombs in the middle of the night when no one is around. They're going to want casualties. A lot of them."

"I've never disarmed a bomb," Ziv said.

"Nor have I," Eben added.

"I'll walk you through it after I see what we've got," X-Ray said. "They probably all have the same triggering and timing system."

"Probably?" Ziv said.

"I've disarmed a hundred bombs and I still have all my appendages," X-Ray said. "Don't worry about it."

"That's easy to say when you'll be walking us through it well out of the blast zone," Eben said.

"Let's get back to the real problem," Vanessa said. "We could be hundreds of miles away from you, Boone, by the time the targets reach their destination. That's going to leave you on your own."

"Not exactly," Boone admitted. "I'm sure Felix will get some wheels, if he hasn't already. And John Masters will be meeting up with me somewhere down the road."

"Have you told John about the car bombs?" Vanessa asked.

"No."

"How about the president?"

"No."

"And?"

"And if I tell him he's going to send in the cavalry."

"That might not be a bad idea."

"We're not ready yet," Boone said. "He has a SEAL team standing by. And if I know J.R., he's already ordered them south so they can get to us quickly if I tell him to pull the trigger. We'll be covered when the time comes. I want you to concentrate on disabling the bombs. I have it covered down here. I'll keep you posted. You do the same."

He ended the call.

I stared out the side window at the trees whipping back and forth. Angela returned to the kitchen table and was staring at the laptop. Boone stared out the windshield at the Tahoe in the distance. Croc jumped back onto the leather sofa and started chasing a flea on his nether region.

The itch.

I took my cards out and started shuffling. I wasn't exactly sure how to ease back into the conversation I wanted to have with Boone when deaf Felix nearly flipped us. *Hey Boone, as I was saying before we found out about the car bombs, and it's very likely the president's daughter is in the Tahoe we're following, and the only help you have are two kids and a toothless dog, but I wanted to talk to you about this thing I get that I call "the itch."*

I split the deck with one hand, twenty-six cards in each stack, then split it again, then made four perfect fans of thirteen cards each, then folded them back into a complete deck without changing the order of a single card, then I started again.

"Something on your mind?" Boone asked.

Before I could answer, a flash of light in the side-view mirror caught my attention. It caught Boone's attention too.

"What the . . ."

There was a car on our tail, flashing its brights on and off.

"Felix?" I asked.

"Not unless he hijacked a jet from the Cracker Barrel," Boone said. "Whoever it is, if they keep it up, they're going to tip off the Tahoe."

"It's passing us," Angela said. She was on her feet, looking out the kitchen window.

Boone let up on the gas so the car could pass more easily, but the car didn't pass. It matched our speed and began honking its horn. I undid my seat belt and leaned over to look.

It was the yellow Hummer.

The Hummer

"What's he trying to do?" Boone shouted. "Who is he?"

"He's my dad," I said.

Angela joined us up front. "He's supposed to be at Rehab Rock," Angela said.

"Can't believe everything you read in the papers."

"What are you two talking about?" Boone asked.

I told him about seeing the Hummer earlier.

"Are you sure it's him?"

"I am now," I said.

"What's he doing here?"

"I don't know."

"Well, he's going to ruin everything."

"He usually does," I said, feeling terrible even though it wasn't my fault he was there.

"Maybe it's a Match groupie who recognized the coach," Angela said.

I shook my head. The itch. I should have never doubted it. "My dad is in the yellow Hummer honking at us and he's not going to stop until you let me out."

"Let you out?" Boone asked.

"It's the only way. And you need to do it right now." I pointed through the windshield. The Tahoe taillights were no longer in view.

Boone stared at the dark road ahead.

"My dad's nuts," I said. "But he's harmless . . . except to himself. I'll find out what he wants. I'll slow him down, or get him out of here. We can't sacrifice the president's daughter for Speed Paulsen."

"I'll pull over and talk to him," Boone said, letting up on the gas.

"There's no time!" I said. "Just drop me off and go. You need to catch up with the Tahoe."

Boone gave me a grim nod, slowed, and started to pull off onto the shoulder. The Hummer dropped back behind us.

"Take Angela's phone. I'll have Felix pick you up and talk to your dad on his way south."

That ought to be an interesting conversation, I thought as I grabbed my coat and Angela's phone. I was out the door before the coach came to a complete stop. Boone was back on the interstate and heading south before I could turn around and look at the Hummer. Croc was standing next to me. I was surprised. I hadn't seen him jump out. The wind blew the rain sideways. No one got out of the Hummer. It just sat there twenty feet away with steam rising off the hood. What if it wasn't my dad? I looked south again. The coach disappeared around a curve. I was getting drenched, but I didn't move. I wanted to give the coach as big of a head start as possible. Croc was looking up at me like I had lost my mind. But he didn't know what I knew. My dad had ombrophobia. Speed was afraid of rain. That wasn't exactly accurate. There was more to it. He didn't like being out in the rain, or being splashed in a pool, or being squirted with a squirt gun, which I did to him when I was a kid, and watched in horror as he grabbed the gun from me and jumped up and down on it until it was a pile of red plastic dust. His paranoia about getting splashed was a family secret. It was one of the few things the press didn't know about him. I was now convinced the guy behind the wheel was my dad. I could have stood there all night long, and as long as it was raining, he would not get out of the Hummer.

But if he got frustrated enough, he might run me over. I hadn't been exactly truthful with Boone when I told him my dad was harmless. He had never hurt me, but he had been arrested a couple of times for assault and battery. And then there was the time he tried to smash his way with a baseball bat onto the sailboat mom and I were living on, which led to Mom getting a restraining order against him. I gave it thirty seconds more, then walked around to the passenger side. The passenger window rolled down.

"Hey, Sport," he said. He always called me *Sport.* I'm not sure why. He hated sports. He was leaning as far away from the passenger window as he could. "Why are you standing in the rain, man?"

Definitely my dad. Whether you were a guy, or a girl, or a dog, you were *man.*

"I wasn't sure it was you," I said.

"Why did you think it was me, man?"

This was going to be a lot harder than I thought.

"I thought I saw you at the truck stop, but the Hummer threw me. I've never seen you drive a car. I didn't think you knew how to drive. But when you tried to flag us down, I knew I was wrong about that. Or thought I knew."

He nodded as if that was a reasonable explanation, and to his addled brain it probably was.

"Hop in, man."

I opened the back door for Croc, then climbed into the front seat. This was a mistake. As soon as I closed my door, Croc started shaking the water off. My dad started swearing and nearly went through the roof trying to get away from the splatter. I jumped up from my seat and tried to get Croc to stop, but he was having none of that. He was determined to shed every drop of rain. I swear he was grinning at the chaos he was causing. He hadn't done this when we got back into the coach after spotting the Tahoe, and we were just as wet then. My dad curled up into a ball behind the driver's seat, with his T-shirt pulled up over his head, stringing together curse words that made absolutely no sense next to each other. After what seemed like an eternity, Croc turned the shower off and laid down as if nothing had happened.

"Sorry," I said. "I didn't know he was going to do that."

Dad was either too shook up to speak, or else he didn't hear me above his rapid-fire cursing. Eventually he ran out of steam, and strange word combinations, and popped his head out of his T like a turtle. He ran his hands through his shoulder-length hair, checking for damp spots.

"What's the deal with the dog, man?" he asked.

"He's not mine. He jumped out when I did."

He glanced back at Croc. Croc gave him a deep growl.

"Is that Tyrone's dog?"

"You know Boone?"

"Everybody knows Tyrone Boone, man. I thought he'd been moldering in the grave by now. It blew my mind when I saw him outside the White House."

"You were in D.C.?"

"Tried to get into the concert there, but of course the Secret Service gestapo wouldn't let me in."

"It was invitation only," I said. Angela and I had passed out a lot of those invitations. If I'd known he wanted to go, I wouldn't have given him one either. With his arrest record, they wouldn't have let him in anyway, invitation or not.

"I tried to catch you in Philly, but missed you. So I borrowed this yellow monstrosity from a friend and drove down. I waited for you to leave the White House, and decided to follow and catch you at your next stop. Lost you for a bit, because I had to stop and fill this yellow pig with gas."

There were some major holes in his story, but there were going to be even bigger holes in my story once I figured what my story was going to be. I wasn't there to pick his story apart. I was there to stop him from following the coach so Boone could follow the Tahoe. The longer I could keep him on the shoulder shooting the breeze, the less chance he'd have wrecking Operation Medusa.

He looked down the dark road, tapping his ringed fingers on the steering wheel to the rhythm of the windshield wiper. Busy hands. He didn't know what to do with them without a guitar. Wonder where my busy hands came from?

... *tap* ... *tap* ... *tap* ...

"I guess your mom and what's-his-name aren't in the coach."

He knew that what's-his-name was Roger Tucker, but I didn't call him on it. "Yeah, they're still at the White House. They're doing a press conference with the president tomorrow for the bombing victims' relief fund."

"The bombs." ... *tap* ... *tap* ... *tap* ... "That was a bummer, man."

I nodded in agreement and thought about the other bombs rolling down the road to kill people.

... *tap* ... *tap* ... *tap* ...

"The reason I knew your mom wasn't in the coach was that you jumped, and it took off like a shot. No way she'd let you do that if she was inside. What was that all about?"

... *tap* ... *tap* ...

Here we go, I thought. *It's whopper time.*

"The second tour truck broke down on its way south. Boone had to head down to see what he could do to get it moving again. Angela and I decided to ride with him. We were getting kind of bored in the White House. Mom and Roger are flying down to the next gig."

... *tap* ... *tap* ... *tap* ... *tap* ... *tap* ...

"You'd think Boone would have at least made sure it was me before dumping you out in the middle of nowhere, man."

I lost track of how many taps it took me to come up with an explanation for this.

"He didn't want to stop at all," I said. "He's trying to beat the hurricane so he doesn't get hung up. No truck, no concert. He was kind of in a panic."

. . . *tap* . . . *tap* . . .

"Thought their next gig was in San Antonio. Weird way to get down to Texas from D.C."

I shrugged. "I'm just along for the ride. I don't pick the routes. Boone doesn't explain much. Angela wanted to jump off with me, but thought she should stay to keep Boone from falling asleep and driving off the road. The guy's pretty old."

"Ancient, man." . . . *tap* . . . "Surprised he still has a license, man. Tell your mom I can get you a better driver. She's gonna want a different driver when she finds out he dumped you and drove away."

"I'll tell her."

He stopped tapping and put the Hummer into gear. "Ready to go, man?"

"Go where?"

"Catch your ride before he gets too far ahead."

"Maybe we could go back to D.C. and I can fly down with Mom tomorrow."

"I'm your dad, not your chauffeur." He pulled the Hummer out onto the highway and started south. "I'm heading down to the Florida Keys. The only reason I stopped in D.C. was because it was on my way."

I doubted that was the only reason. Mom thought he'd show up somewhere on the tour, and she wasn't looking forward to it. I looked at the speedometer. He was going eighty miles an hour. At that rate, it wouldn't take him too long to catch up to the coach. Then what?

"What are you going to do in Florida?" I asked, hoping to distract him and maybe slow him down.

"The guy that owns this hog has a place in Largo. I'm going to chill for a couple of weeks. Write some new tunes. Get some alone time."

Alone time? I wondered again if this was really my dad. I was seeing a side of him I'd never seen before—a side I suspected no one had ever seen. He looked like my dad and talked like my dad, but he wasn't acting like my dad. He was driving a Hummer. He wanted alone time? The speedometer dropped down to seventy-six miles an hour.

"Speaking of tunes," he said, "how's that album of your mom's doing?"

First, it wasn't my mom's album, it was Roger and Mom's album. Second, he knew very well how their album was doing. Everyone in the music business knew the Match album and their single "Rekindled" were well on their way to going platinum.

"I don't know," I lied.

"And she remarried, huh?"

Another lie. Mom's marriage to what's-his-name at Golden Gate Park in San Francisco had gotten the royal wedding treatment around the world. You would have had to be dead not to have at least heard about it.

"Yeah," I said.

"What's the stepfather like?"

I shrugged noncommittally, even though I liked Roger a lot, except for his vegetarianism.

He gave me a sympathetic look, then reached over and

squeezed my shoulder. "Give him time, man," he said sagely.

It was all I could do not to burst out in laughter. But it did slow him down to seventy-three miles an hour, and there was still no sign of the coach.

"I thought I read somewhere that you were on the Rock."

Seventy miles an hour.

"I was . . . for about five minutes. In the front door, out the back. It was the only way I could figure out how to hit the road for a couple of weeks for some incognito. Good advertisement for the rehab facility, and good for me. I've been clean for . . . well . . . for days."

I didn't know if that was true or not, but he did seem pretty lucid for him. There were times in my life where he had looked at me blankly as if he didn't know who I was. The incognito thing was one of his pipe dreams. He hadn't done anything to disguise himself. Everyone knew what Speed Paulsen looked like, and to top it off he was driving an SUV that shouted: "Look at me, man!" I was surprised there wasn't a mile-long line of paparazzi and fans following us.

The speedometer was back up to eighty miles an hour.

Angela's cell phone rang. It was Boone.

"You okay?" he asked.

I glanced over at Dad. "Yeah. We're behind you."

"Maybe not. The Tahoe just turned off I-95 onto 64 East. Have you passed it yet?"

"I don't think so."

"What's your dad up to?"

"He's headed to the Florida Keys."

Dad looked over at me. I smiled. "It's Boone."

"'Bout time he checked in to see if you were alive, man."

"What did you tell him?" Boone asked.

"Yeah, I told him about the second tour truck breaking down," I said.

Boone didn't say anything for a second or two. I wondered if I'd screwed up.

"Tell him you were mistaken," he finally said. "Tell him it was an accident, not a breakdown. Tell him there were injuries. Tell him I'm headed to the hospital to check on the drivers before I check on the truck."

"What about—" I stopped myself just in time. Some secret agent I'd make.

Dad pulled into the left lane to pass a slow semi-truck in the right lane. Croc started barking, then jumped into the far back and began scratching at the window.

"Tell him to knock that off!" Dad shouted.

I scrambled into the backseat and grabbed Croc's collar. He growled, and for a second I thought he was going to bite me, or gum me.

"What's the matter with you!"

Croc continued to growl. I held on to his collar in one hand and the phone in the other.

"You there, Boone?"

"What's going on?" Boone asked.

"Croc freaked out. He's okay now." I looked at him. "I think."

"There's a hospital on the right-hand side of 64, not far from the interchange. The coach will be locked. Go into admissions. Angela will be in the waiting room. If your dad comes in with you, you'll have to ditch him."

"What about . . . ?" Once again I couldn't finish the question without tipping my dad, but I didn't want them to lose the Tahoe because of me.

"We caught a break," Boone said. "John Masters showed up. He's behind the Tahoe. We'll catch up to him down the road. I have another call coming in. See you at the hospital."

He ended the call. I climbed back into the front seat. Croc had stopped growling, but he stayed where he was, staring out the back window.

"Well?" Dad asked.

"I guess it wasn't a breakdown," I said. "It was an accident. The drivers are in the hospital. Boone is going to meet me there." I was surprised at how easily the lie flowed out of my mouth.

Dad nodded. "Where's the hospital?"

"Up ahead off 64."

He nodded again as if he knew where that was, which was surprising, because the dad I knew couldn't find his way around his own mansion without a guide.

I was still feeling the itch . . . at least I thought it was the itch. It could have been my wet clothes drying in the hot Hummer, but I didn't think so. When the premonition comes true or shows up like this one, the itch goes away. It's like someone walking up and scratching your back where you can't reach. I looked over at my dad. He was staring down the road, tapping the steering wheel to a tune only he could hear. I turned my head and looked at Croc. He was still in the back looking out the rear window. And that's when I knew. The itch hadn't been caused by my unexpected appearance—not entirely anyway.

The thing at the rest area was like the three-cup magic trick, but it was done with four Tahoes instead of three cups, and sixteen people instead of three balls. Sixteen people had pulled into the rest area, but there were already two people there. Sixteen people left in the four Tahoes, but they weren't the same sixteen people. They had made a switch.

I turned again to look at Croc. He was still in the back, but he was no longer looking out the window. He was staring at me, his weird blue eye drilling into me like he was reading my mind. Behind him the road was black. No sign of the eighteen-wheeler Croc had been barking at. I hadn't thought to look at the side of the truck, but I was certain there was a giant red crab on it with The Maryland Fish Company below.

The itch was gone.

Malak and Bethany were behind us.

Left Turn

The semi-trailer smelled like old fish and rattled like a thunderclap with no end.

When they were switched to the semi at the rest area, Malak thought about shooting Scuffed Boots and his partner, ending the operation right there. But she thought better of it when she saw how gently Scuffed Boots handled the yoga-breathing Bethany Culpepper. He picked her up, still wrapped in the tarp, and laid her in the back of the truck as if he was afraid to wake her.

"You're supposed to ride back here," he said apologetically and with a certain amount of fear. The deference and fear didn't surprise Malak. She had grown to expect this from people who learned she was Anmar, the Leopard.
Like she had with Willing and Able, she wanted to ask him where he was taking them, but didn't because that would show weakness. It would tell him that she didn't know where they were going, and this would tell him that she wasn't in the upper echelon of the cell.

"I know exactly where we are supposed to be," she said. "And we're behind schedule."

"I'll need that disposable cell back," he said.

She tossed it to him without complaint, happy he hadn't asked her for her gun. She climbed into the back. Scuff Boots closed her and Bethany into the pitch-dark metal box. She waited until they were moving before she uncovered Bethany and removed the hood.

"Are you okay?" She had to raise her voice to be heard above the thunderous rattle.

Bethany sat up.

"That yoga breath works pretty good," Malak said.

"I'll give you a lesson when this is all over."

"I could use it," Malak said, hoping they were both still breathing when this was all over.

"Where are we?" Bethany asked.

"We're in the back of a semi-truck."

"I know we're in a truck," Bethany said. "What I want to know is where we are geographically."

"I'm sorry," Malak said. "I think we're heading south on I-95 toward the North Carolina border."

"What do you mean *you think*?"

Malak could hear the panic in her voice. She found Bethany's hand and began to brief the president's daughter. She told her about the discovery of her identical twin sister and her sister's death at Independence Hall. She told her about the ghost cell and becoming Anmar, the Leopard. She told her about her kidnapping and the SOS team. When she finished, Bethany lay completely still. Malak couldn't tell if she had heard her or not. She couldn't see her. She couldn't see her own hand in front of her face. The only visible light was from the luminous hands of her Seamaster watch. She wished now that she hadn't taken out the tracking device J.R. had put in it. She pulled Q's iPhone out of her pocket and hit the wake button. Nothing happened. She hit again. The screen was as black as the inside of the truck. The phone would have given them a little light, but more importantly it was their only tie to the SOS team. She doubted the team had caught the switch at the rest area. Not keeping the disposable cell phone had been a terrible mistake. The Leopard could not afford to make mistakes.

Bethany finally spoke, but her words were lost in the noise of the trailer. Malak leaned in closer. "I didn't hear."

"You've sacrificed so much," Bethany repeated, squeezing her hand.

Malak closed her eyes, happy for the dark now, so Bethany could not see her trying to hold back tears. She *had* sacrificed a lot the past four years. Seeing Angela in Philadelphia and D.C. had reminded her just how much this fight had cost her. If she didn't discover the leader of the ghost cell and take him out, it would all have been for nothing.

"I'm sorry you're involved in this," Malak said.

"I probably wouldn't have volunteered for it," Bethany said. "And my dad would have never allowed it, even if I was crazy enough to say I'd do it. But now that I'm here I'm . . ."

The vehicle slowed. They grabbed on to each other to

stop themselves from slipping across the wooden floor. The truck came to a stop, swung to the left, then accelerated again.

"We've left the interstate," Malak said. "We're heading west."

Incognito

The last time I'd been to a hospital Angela had shattered someone's knee and cracked Eben Lavi's tooth with two strategically placed tae kwon do kicks. I was hoping she'd keep her feet to herself this time, because Eben had paid her back by sticking a knife in my neck. It wasn't a pleasant experience. I was also hoping that my dad would drop me off at the entrance and continue his trip down to the Florida Keys without looking back. No such luck. As soon as we pulled into the parking lot, he spotted the coach and made a beeline for it.

"They're not in the coach," I said. "They're in the hospital. You can just drop me out front."

"I'm not going to just dump you off like your worthless roadie did, man. If he's not in the coach, I'll go inside the hospital with you to find him. Is what's-his-name's daughter traveling with you?"

I'd already told him that she was and if he knew what's-his-name had a daughter, then he knew what's-his-name was Roger Tucker, and probably everything else about him, and Mom, and the band, and how their album was doing on Billboard.

"Angela," I said. "She's with us."

He parked the Hummer in front of the coach. "How's that going, man?" he asked.

"How's what going?"

"The daughter, man. What's she like?"

I wanted to tell him that she could kick his teeth out and that her mother was a notorious terrorist.

"She's okay," I said. "We get along." I didn't want to tell him that I actually liked Angela quite a bit. That what we had been through together in the last few days had made us more than brother and sister. That I'd do anything for her and thought she'd do anything for me.

"That's cool," he said, and shut the engine off. He looked at the coach through the window.

The coach was dark. The wind was blowing. It was raining.

"See if they're in there," he said.

"They aren't. Boone's checking on the drivers."

"Just check, man. You gotta key?"

"There's a spare in a hide-a-key in the wheel well."

I opened the door. Croc was over the front seat and out before I could take my hand off the handle. I thought about how he had caught up to me on the overpass. I guess he was quicker and more agile than he looked.

"I'll wait here," Dad said, ridiculously.

Of course you're going to wait here. It's raining. You have ombrophobia. Which is going to work to my advantage. Shouldn't be too hard to ditch someone who can't go outside. But not yet and not here. We aren't going anywhere with the Hummer parked next to the coach. The ditching will have to take place somewhere else.

I jumped out. Croc wasn't anywhere to be seen.

He's probably looking for a good tire to pee on. He'll show up at the right place at the right time, like Boone always does. That's one thing they have in common. That and their uncanny ability to sniff out terrorists. How'd Croc know that Malak and Bethany were in the fish truck going seventy miles an hour? How'd I know that? Did I know that? I mean, did I really know they were inside? Maybe Boone and Croc have itches too. Croc's always scratching himself. How am I going to explain the itch to Boone? He'll think I'm crazy. He'll . . .

"Stop!" I yelled, and nearly grabbed my head to still my thoughts.

I didn't have time for a brain race. I needed to ditch my dad. We needed to get back on the road and find that truck. I hurried over to the coach door. It was locked. I knocked to make it look good in case my dad was watching, which I was sure he was. No one answered. Big surprise. I thought about grabbing the spare key and looking inside, but what was the point? I jogged back to the Hummer and opened the passenger door.

"They aren't there," I shouted above the wind. "I'll just run over to the hospital. Great seeing you."

"I'll drive you," he said. "Hop in."

It would take me twice as long to argue with him than it would for him to drive me the two hundred feet to the entrance. I hopped in. But he didn't drive to the entrance. He drove into a parking structure. It took us forever to find a spot because the Hummer was so big.

We got out, walked into the hospital, and began winding our way down long hallways and steep stairways. There weren't too many people around this time of night. Most of them were sleepy-looking nurses, doctors, and technicians wearing pink, blue, or green scrubs. Not surprisingly, we got some double takes as we made our way, but no one stopped us or said anything. I got the feeling that Dad was a little disappointed by this. He wasn't exactly trying to hide who he was as he clacked down the hallways in his ten-thousand-dollar snakeskin cowboy boots. His hair was halfway down his back, highlighted with red and gold streaks and carefully placed exotic bird feathers. I hadn't noticed it in the Hummer, but he was wearing about eighteen pounds of gold around his neck and a diamond in his ear big enough to buy a hospital wing. Couple this with his thousand-dollar pair of jeans, professionally ripped and torn in all the right places, and his orange silk T-shirt, he was the exact opposite of incognito. He looked like he was back stage at a sold-out arena waiting to make his guitar sing for his screaming fans.

We finally found our way down to admissions. Angela was sitting in the waiting room with her ratty pack, which looked like it was ready to burst at the seams. What did she have in there?

Dad gave her a big capped-toothed white smile. She returned it and put out her hand. Dad sidestepped the hand and moved in for a big hug. She was startled. I should have warned her that he was a serial hugger, although he hadn't hugged me when I got into the Hummer, but that was probably because I was wet.

He broke off and looked at her. "I'm Speed Paulsen."

"I can see that," Angela said.

Everybody could see it. And I suddenly knew how I was going to ditch him. I was going to use the one thing he craved more than junk food.

He looked around the waiting room. We were the only people there.

"Where's Boone?" he asked.

"He's checking on the drivers," Angela answered without missing a beat.

"At this time of night? Kind of late for visiting hours."

There was a definite pause after this question. An uncomfortably long beat with Angela just staring at him. I jumped in.

"He's probably talking to the doctor, trying to figure out when they're getting out."

Dad nodded as if that was reasonable, then looked back at Angela. "Bad accident?"

"I guess. I mean, the drivers are in the hospital."

"When did it happen?"

"This afternoon." Angela glanced at the clock on the wall. It was a little after 3:00 a.m., and corrected herself. "I mean yesterday afternoon."

"Where?"

"South of here on I-95. I guess the trailer and all the equipment is okay, but the tractor is a wreck. Boone has another tractor on the way, but it won't be here for a couple hours."

Dad's cell phone rang. The ringtone was one of his most famous guitar riffs. He pulled it out, looked at the screen, and frowned. "I better get this." He walked over to the farthest corner of the waiting room.

"Where's Boone?" I asked quietly.

Angela shook her head. "I don't know. He had me grab a bunch of stuff from the coach and told me to meet you in here. We're supposed to meet him out front as soon as we get rid of your dad."

That explained the bursting pack. But why not leave the stuff in the coach?

"I don't know about getting rid of him," I said. "But I think I have a way of distracting him long enough for us to sneak out of here." I looked over at Speed. He was still on the phone. "If he comes back before I get back, tell him I went to the restroom."

"What are you going to do?"

"I'm going to get him a cheeseburger."

"I doubt the cafeteria is open this time of morning."

"It's not that kind of cheeseburger."

I left her there with her mouth open and walked out to the admissions area. The woman in pink scrubs sitting behind the admissions counter was one of the many who had given us the eyeball as we walked past. She wasn't alone. She was talking to a man and another woman, both in scrubs, and all three of them looked at me when I came out. I gave them a friendly smile and a nod, then wandered over to the front doors as if I were checking out the storm. I stretched my arms as if I were stiff, then wandered over to them.

"Heck of a storm," I said.

"The worst has passed," the man said. His name badge said Dan. "It's been downgraded from a hurricane to a tropical storm. There's been some damage on the Outer Banks to the west of us, but nothing too serious." He waved his hand at the empty admissions area. "As you can see, if it was really bad out there we'd have a full house."

"I guess you're right," I said.

"What brings you in?" the woman behind the counter asked. Her name badge said Betty. "Is someone you know here?"

I gave her a sheepish smile. "Actually no. My dad and I were heading down to Florida. He got a little sleepy and wanted to get out and stretch his legs and wake up a little bit. Everything else was closed so we pulled in here. I hope that's okay."

"Better than nodding off and getting into an accident," the second woman, Mary, said.

"We call that preventative medicine," Dan said.

They all laughed.

"I noticed your dad when you walked by," Betty said.

"He's kind of hard not to notice," I said.

This got another laugh.

"He kind of looks like Speed Paulsen," Betty said.

"I'm glad to hear that," I said. "Because he *is* Speed Paulsen."

"I knew it!" Betty said.

"He thought it was a little weird that no one said anything to him," I said.

"We like to give people their privacy," Mary said.

"If someone was visiting a loved one, that makes sense," I said. "But Dad and I are just here to wake up and get out of the rain. Dad's just the opposite of private."

"It must be interesting to have Speed Paulsen as a dad."

"It's more than interesting," I said.

"I'm a huge fan," Dan said. "I have every one of his albums on my iPod. I listen to him all the time."

"You should go in and tell him. He loves meeting fans and talking to them. I'm sure he'd sign an autograph for you, or for anyone else that wants one. He didn't come in here incognito. In fact, talking to him might help him wake up." I looked at my watch. "We probably won't be here too long, so if you want to say hello . . ."

"Does he drink coffee?" Betty asked.

"Are you kidding? Dad loves coffee."

"Lattes?" Betty asked.

"You have a latte maker?"

"The doctors do, up on the second floor. I'll order one right up. I bet he has some fans up there too."

"That would be great," I said. I had no idea if Dad liked lattes or not. Betty picked up the phone.

I turned to Dan and Mary. "Do you want to meet my dad?"

They did. I led them into the waiting room. Dad had finished his call and was standing next to Angela. It was time to see how serious he was about his alone time. Time to see if Dad was hungry.

"I have a couple of people that want to meet you," I said.

Dad's eyes lit up. His smile broadened. He stepped forward and gave Dan, then Mary hugs. Mary's hug was a lot longer than Dan's.

"I love your music," Dan said.

"And I love you for saying that, man."

Another hug for Dan. Four more scrub-clad hospital workers came in. A couple of minutes later, Betty joined them, carrying the latte like a golden goblet, followed by a half dozen more scrubs. My dad took the paper cup and thanked her by kissing her on the lips.

The only thing my dad likes more than junk food is attention. Pink, blue, green—a feast of fans were pouring into the room, making me wonder who was looking after the patients. It was MacPeople time.

I motioned to Angela to get her things. Dad had finished hugging and kissing the first course and had started telling a road-tour story I'd heard a hundred times before. Angela and I backed our way out of the crowd. I looked back as we squeezed through the jammed doorway. Dad wasn't paying any attention to us. He looked like he was enjoying himself. He was the brightest flower in the center of a pastel bouquet of scrubs.

Old Dog, New Tricks

"Cheeseburger, huh?" Angela said as we stepped outside.

"More like a people burger. And we need to get out of here before the restaurant closes."

The coach was easy to spot in the windblown parking lot. It hadn't moved. The windows were still dark.

"What's your dad doing here?"

"He followed us from D.C. He's on his way to Florida. Let's head over to the coach." I stepped off the curb.

"Wait."

I stopped. "What?"

"Boone said to wait here for him."

"My dad's going to ask them about the bogus accident and the phantom drivers. When he finds out that the accident never happened, he's going to come looking for me. And he'll have help. By now every scrub in the hospital thinks they're Speed's best friend. It won't take them long to find me standing out here in the open. We can meet him at the coa—"

A late-model Audi sedan pulled up. Black. Wet. Croc was

in the passenger seat, staring out the window with his tongue hanging out.

"Shotgun," I said.

"The front seat is already taken," Angela said.

"Doesn't apply to dogs."

"Whatever," Angela said, tossing her pack into the backseat.

I opened the front door and told Croc to get into the back. He gave me a dirty look, but squeezed through the seats and joined Angela. Boone peeled out before I got my seat belt on. Bare wires dangled from the steering column. I guess all spies know how to hot-wire cars. For them the world was one huge, used car lot.

"What's your dad's story?" Boone asked.

I told him what I knew, or at least what Dad had told me about why he happened to be on I-95.

"Interesting," Boone said.

"My dad's not fond of cops, but I think he'll call them when he finds out we aren't there."

"It's a big hospital," Boone said. "It will take him a while to figure out we've flown the coop."

"I'm more worried about him calling your mom," Angela said. "If my dad and she think we're in trouble, they'll call the cops."

"I don't think he has Mom's new cell phone number," I said. "And even if he did, I don't think she'd take his call."

"It's covered," Boone said. "Marie and Art are screening all of their calls. Incoming and outgoing."

Marie and Art were part of the SOS team. They were

posing as personal assistants to Mom and Roger.

"You're tapping their phones?" I asked, surprised. But I guess I should have known.

"Isn't that illegal?" Angela asked.

"Yup," Boone admitted. "Legality has never been our strong suit. And that's not the only fail-safe we have in regard to Speed. I disabled his Hummer. He won't be driving it anytime soon. And Felix is back on the road. He's going to stop at the hospital and pick up the coach. When he's there, he'll make sure your dad stays out of the picture."

"What do you mean by 'out of the picture'?" This had frightening implications, especially with Felix doing the keeping him out of the picture. My dad and I had our little problems, but I didn't want him *permanently* out of the picture.

Boone laughed. "Don't worry. Felix is subtler than he looks. And he's not an assassin."

The four vaporized terrorists north of us would probably disagree, I thought.

"The hospital stop is going to work to our advantage," Boone continued. "It's one thing to have a coach dogging you on a major interstate, it's another thing to leave the interstate and have that same coach behind you. I've been thinking about switching vehicles the past hundred miles. With Felix right behind us and Masters just ahead behind the Tahoe, we're back in business."

"Except for the fact that Malak and Bethany aren't in the Tahoe," I said.

Angela leaned up between the seats. Boone glared at me, swerved, then put his eyes back on the road. Croc took advantage of the space in back by stretching out and letting out a satisfied groan.

"What are you talking about?" Angela asked. "If they aren't in the other Tahoes, they have to be in the one we're following."

"It was a trick," I said. "There were at least two people waiting for them at the rest area. Maybe more. It's like the ball and cup trick, but instead of cups and balls, they used Tahoes and at least eighteen people, not sixteen like we thought."

"Are you okay?" Angela asked.

She'd really think I was nuts if I told her why I really thought there had been a switch. Instead, I explained how the trick worked, which wasn't easy without the balls and cups. When I finished, there was dead silence except for Croc's panting.

"How do you know this?" Boone finally asked.

I knew the question was coming, but it still hit me by surprise. I didn't know what to say. If I tried to explain the itch, Boone would probably do a U-turn and check me into the hospital's psyche ward for observation.

"Does Croc have road rage?" I asked.

Boone looked straight ahead. Angela shook her head with a look of pity.

I looked back at Croc. He had his head up and an ear cocked in my direction.

"Explain," Boone said.

Angela just stared at me, apparently too stunned to speak.

I told them about Croc barking at the fish truck when we were Tahoe spotting.

Angela found her voice. "So you're basing your theory on an old dog barking at an eighteen-wheeler barreling down a freeway at seventy miles an hour?"

"Yeah," I said defensively. "And he freaked out again when my dad passed another semi-truck, or maybe the same semi-truck, farther south."

And I get this thing I call the Itch, which is some kind of psychic ability. Something my hero, Erik Weisz (aka Harry Houdini), spent a good part of his life debunking.

But of course I didn't tell her this part.

"What do you mean it might have been the same truck?" Boone asked.

"I didn't put two and two together until we were past it. I couldn't very well tell my dad to slow down so I could read the side of a truck."

"I guess not," Boone said.

"You're not really buying into this," Angela said. "Croc is a dog."

"Actually I am completely buying into it," Boone said.

"How could Croc possibly know what was in that truck?" Angela was leaning so far forward, I thought she was going to climb into the front with us.

"Croc is a remarkable dog," Boone answered. "With unusual abilities."

"We need to stick to the Tahoe," Angela insisted.

Boone did not respond. Instead he called Felix and piped the conversation through the Audi's sound system.

"Where are you?" Boone asked.

"Ninety-five. Ten minutes from 64."

"Bypass 64," Boone said. "Stay on 95. We're looking for an eighteen-wheeler. Maryland Fish Company. Big red crab on the trailer."

"What's inside?"

"Our two friends."

"How do you know?"

"Croc."

"Okay," Felix said.

Apparently Boone wasn't the only one who thought Croc was remarkable.

"The truck could be anywhere," Boone said. "I'd stay on 95 for a hundred miles or so. If you don't see it, turn back."

Speed was safe from a Big Felix encounter, at least for a while.

"Got a Benz now," Felix said.

Used car lot, I thought.

Felix ended the call.

Angela pushed Super Dog over and slumped back into her seat.

Boone glanced at her in the rearview mirror. "Don't look so glum. We'll continue on 64 until we find the truck or catch up with the Tahoe. We have to find both of them. The Tahoe may have a bomb in it."

He called John Masters.

Supercenter

"Got it," John said. "Red crab, Maryland Fish Company. I've passed seven semi-trucks, but none matching that description."

The moment he had gotten off the phone with the president, his years of SEAL training had kicked in. He could have given Boone a list of every make and model of every car and truck he had seen in the past hour, along with a pretty good guess as to how many people were inside the vehicles. He was pleased that his years in construction hadn't deconstructed his skill as an operative.

Like riding a bicycle.

I hope.

He stared down the road at the Tahoe's taillights. Two tiny red dots moving through the night.

"What makes you think they're inside that truck?" he asked.

There was a noticeable pause before Boone answered. "You don't want to know."

Actually John *did* want to know, but he let it go. Something else was bothering him.

"I don't think there's a bomb in this Tahoe," he said.

"Why?" Boone asked.

"If they keep heading east, they're going to run into the Outer Banks and the Atlantic Ocean. There's nothing to blow up out there but sand and vacation homes. I just drove through there on my way down here."

"Reasonable," Boone said. "What's your point?"

"If you're convinced that Bethany and Malak are in the fish truck, then who's in the Tahoe? Where are they going? What do you think they're doing?"

"If they head north when they get to the Outer Banks, they could be taking a roundabout way to Norfolk. Plenty of civilian and military targets up there, but I see what you're getting at. Regardless of who's in the Tahoe, we still need to tail it to the end point and make sure it's clean. Any chance of getting a visual of the occupants?"

"Short of running them off the road, negative. Too dark to do a drive-by through this section. Wait a second . . ." John leaned forward in order to see better through the rain-spattered windshield. "I have a right-turn signal. They're taking the exit up ahead. I'll get back to you."

He clicked off and slowed down. He needed to be close enough to see which way they turned after they took the exit, but far enough behind so they didn't see him take the exit. Halfway up the ramp he switched off his headlights so they wouldn't detect his turn, but as he made the turn at the top, he discovered the precaution hadn't been necessary. The road to the right was as straight as a ruler for as far as he could see. The Tahoe was not on it.

He didn't panic. The Tahoe could not have gone very far, but he was worried about countersurveillance. He knew that the best way to find out if you're being followed is to pull off the road and see if someone comes by, acting like they're looking for you. He turned his headlights back on as he eased around the corner. A passing car without headlights in the middle of the night was a dead giveaway. So was a car crawling along at twenty miles an hour.

He stepped on the gas, just enough to make it look like he was on his way somewhere, but not so fast that he couldn't scan right and left for the Tahoe. He found it parked among a half dozen other cars in a Wal-Mart Supercenter. It was open twenty-four hours a day. Open or not, he was surprised to see any cars in the parking lot.

Who goes shopping at three-thirty in the morning in weather like this?

He was about to find out. He continued past the store at the same speed, until he found an inconspicuous spot to pull over. He grabbed the kit bag he'd put together and jogged back up the road. There was a chain restaurant on the south side of the parking lot with a stand of trees to hide behind.

He took out his spotting scope and scanned the parking lot. In addition to the insomniac shoppers' vehicles near the entrance, there were seven RVs parked on his side of the lot.

Three trailers. Four motor homes. All dark. Sleeping. Riding out the storm.

He fixed the scope on the Tahoe. It was empty. He scanned the other vehicles. They were empty too. Inside the store he spotted one person. An employee wearing a Wal-Mart blue apron. She was standing at the only open checkout stand looking bored out of her mind.

So where's everyone else?

Six cars meant a minimum of five customers inside, aside from the terrorists, providing that employees parked around back, which he assumed they did. The terrorists could be meeting someone inside, although that would be risky because of all the surveillance cameras. Bethany Culpepper had one of the most recognizable faces on earth. If they had her, they wouldn't dare walk her through a Wal-Mart.

Boone's right. They don't have Bethany Culpepper. So what are they doing in there?

It could have been something as simple as a restroom stop, but he didn't think so.

The one thing the president hadn't provided for him were credentials, or creds, as they were called. Flashing a federal badge opened a lot of doors. The easiest way to monitor the terrorists would be to get access to the store's surveillance room. But flashing a shield in a nearly empty store at this time of morning would be like getting on the intercom and announcing his arrival.

Attention shoppers and terrorists . . .

All of these thoughts and more flashed through his mind in a matter of seconds, but when it got down to it there were really only two choices.

Watch or move.

John moved.

He figured someone from the Tahoe was running countersurveillance on the parking lot and the entrance to the

Supercenter. That's what he would have done in their place. He stayed behind the trees until he drew even with the parked RVs, then used them to block their view. The trick would be to convince them that he was coming from one of the RVs to do some late-night shopping. He found a perfect spot to make his approach. He used the biggest motor home to make it look like he came from the ratty fifth-wheel trailer parked behind it. It also set him up for a straight-line approach to the Supercenter entrance right past the Tahoe.

It was still pouring out, but the wind had died down some. He put his collar up and pulled his stocking cap down over his ears. He walked quickly, hunched over, as if the last thing he wanted to do was cross the parking lot in miserable weather. As he hurried passed the front of the Tahoe, he slipped something between the grill slats, hoping they didn't discover it.

The pneumatic doors slid open. At this time of morning, there was no cheerful Wal-Mart greeter, but there was a frowning terrorist. He was leaning against the Red Box video dispenser. John had missed him with the scope and he was sure he was out of view of the surveillance camera, which he was sure was there, although he didn't look up to check. Only bad guys, operatives, and cops checked out cameras.

He took off his stocking cap and slapped it on his knee to get some water out, then looked at the guy, smiled, and said, "Wet enough out there for you?"

The guy returned the smile, but his eyes were two blue orbs of glacial ice. His head was shaved. Fair skin. Blond eyebrows. Nordic features. Except for the blinking Bluetooth in his ear, he was nothing like the descriptions of the terrorists in the other Tahoes. He wore a black coat, baggy enough to conceal deadly weapons, but it was clear he needed nothing more than his hands for any threat that might arise. John had seen the look many times before. Fifteen years ago he'd had the same look–completely relaxed, yet ready to pounce and kill. The guy was a professional at the peak of his skill set.

"You come from that caravan?" he asked with a slight New York accent.

You know exactly where I came from. You watched every step I took. But you missed something, pal.

John broadened his smile. "Yeah, I'm in the crappy fifth-wheel. I'm on my way to a job site in the Outer Banks . . . or I was. I'm going to stay parked until this storm blows through. I've had enough of white-knuckle driving."

"Where are you going in OBX?"

"OB what?"

"That's what the locals call the Outer Banks."

"I'm not a local. I've never been there. I'm from Tampa. I'm on my way to a place called Manteo." He glanced into the store. "But right now I'm after a carton of cigarettes."

"Those things can kill you."

So could you. Or you could try.

"Thanks for the reminder." John grabbed a cart and pushed into the store.

He pulled a few things off the shelves that he didn't need or want, to make it look good while he looked for the other terrorists. They weren't hard to pick out from the regular customers. He found T2 in the produce department, sorting through a pile of Red Delicious apples. He could have been T1's brother, except he had blond hair down to his shoulders. T2 glanced at John for a second, then went back to his apples.

Perfect. Don't look for them. Bump into them.

He grabbed a pack of bologna from the cooler, put it in his cart, then continued his terrorist shopping spree.

By the time he bumped into T3 and T4, his cart was half full of things a guy living in a trailer might eat. It wasn't hard for him to pick out the items because he was actually a guy who lived in a trailer.

T3 was a woman. T4 was a man. They were in the bread aisle, topping off their full cart with multigrain loaves of bread. John grabbed a loaf of white bread, tossed it into the cart, then pushed past them as if he were in a hurry. He slowed down in the next aisle over and digested what he had seen. The woman, T3, was in charge, and not just of the shopping—she was in charge of everything. It was clear by how T4 responded to her. When John breezed by, T4 didn't look at him, he looked at her. She had given him a nearly invisible shake of the head, indicating that he should stand down. There was no threat from the trailer guy. The head shake told John something else. This was not the first time T3 and T4, and probably the other two as well, had worked together. They were a team, a crew of highly trained professionals. They had the look of independent operators. They didn't have to make a call to get permission for their next move. If T3 wanted the trailer guy killed, T4 would pop him right next to the white bread. T3 was two inches taller than T4, and John was T4's height. The woman had shiny black hair pulled back in a severe ponytail, a loose fitting coat like the other Ts, and brown eyes that missed nothing . . .

Except for me. Not surprising. Fifteen years out of the game is a pretty good disguise.

He wondered if the woman was Malak Turner. He had no idea what the Leopard looked like. He'd have to have Boone upload a photo of her. If she wasn't the Leopard, who was she? And what about the groceries? This had to be a planned stop. They were stocking up for a long stay someplace.

Why? Where?

He reached the end of the aisle and started up the next, adding a few more random items to his cart. He was in no hurry to leave the store now. There was no need to bump into the terrorists again. He reached the end of the aisle, glanced left, then moved to the next aisle. The terrorists were checking out. He figured they'd be gone by the time he got to the end of the next aisle over. They were. The checker was back to counting the minutes until her shift was over. He pushed his cart down and up two more aisles. His last stop was the tobacco counter, where he added a carton of cigarettes to his pile. He doubted they were watching, but he had to make it look good in case they were.

He pushed the cart up to the lonely checker. She started scanning and dumping items into plastic bags. The final tab came to a little over a hundred dollars. One of the items in the kit the president had provided for him was a bundle of cash. The operation was off the grid. Credit card transactions were traceable. He paid, wheeled the cart to the entrance, but stopped before going out into the rain. As he rummaged through the bags, he glanced out at the cars in the parking lot. The Tahoe was gone, but that didn't mean they weren't watching him. He found the carton of cigarettes, pulled a pack out, unwrapped it, and lit one.

Nasty.

But necessary. The cigarette might just save his life. A guy from a trailer desperate for a cigarette would definitely light up before braving the weather with his groceries. If the terrorists suspected he wasn't who he said he was, they would kill him as he crossed the dark parking lot. He crushed the cigarette out, put on his stocking cap, then pushed the cart through the sliding glass doors hoping there wasn't a sniper bullet waiting for him as he crossed the parking lot.

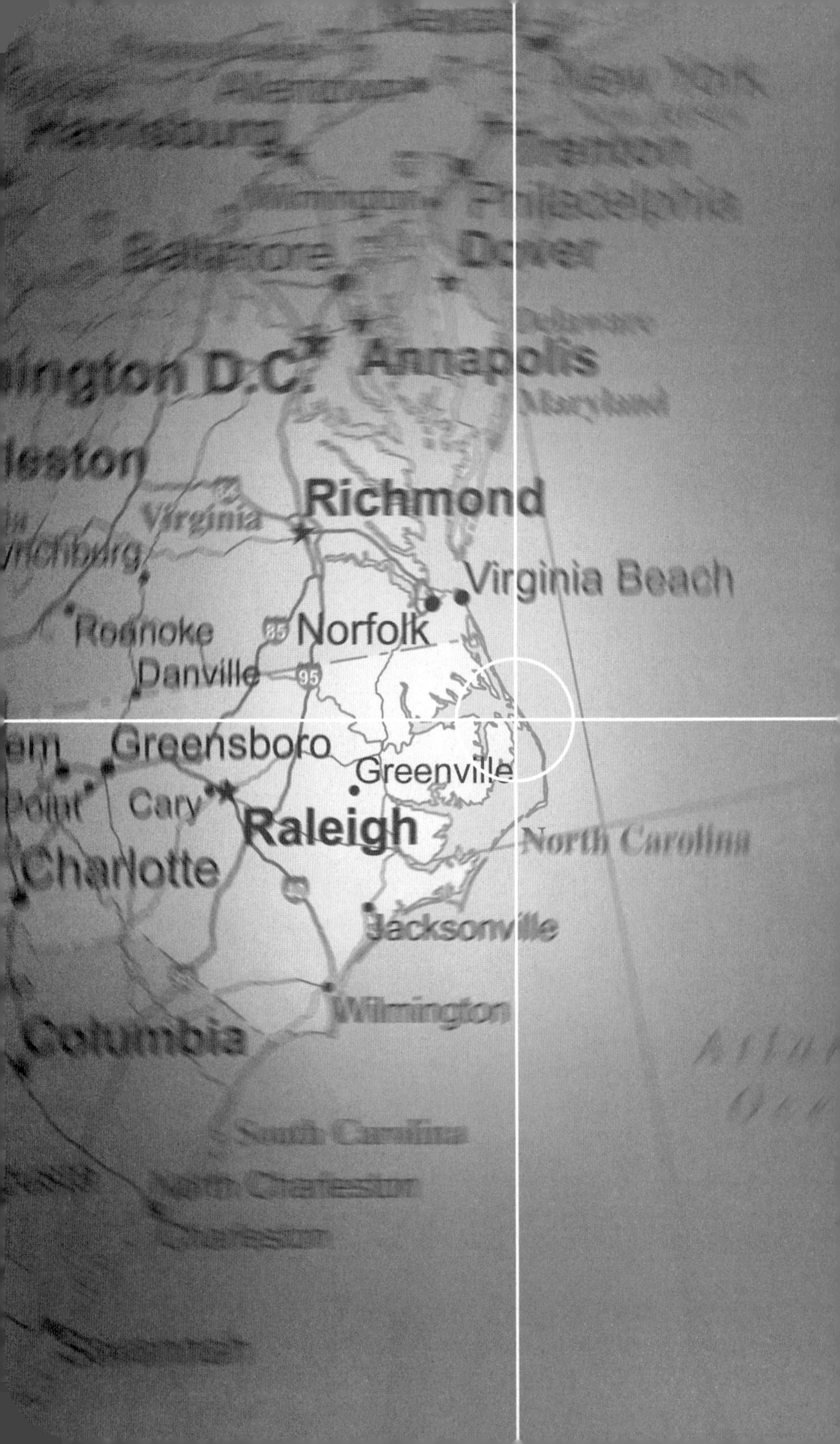
Annapolis
Richmond
Virginia
Virginia Beach
Norfolk
85
95
Roanoke
Danville
Greensboro
Greenville
Cary
Raleigh
Charlotte
North Carolina
Jacksonville
Wilmington
Columbia
South Carolina

SUNDAY, SEPTEMBER 7 >

4:00 a.m. to 6:20 a.m.

Dog Years

I was manipulating cards in the front seat, keeping an eye out for the red crab truck while I listened to Angela giving us a running travelogue about the Outer Banks, which she was cobbling together from the web. I'm not sure why she was doing this. There was better than a fifty-fifty chance that the crab truck was rolling down I-95 and we'd be turning around. I guess the travelogue was her version of manipulating cards. She was nervous. Busy lips.

"Virginia Dare was the first child born in America to English parents. August 18, 1587. She was born in the Roanoke Colony on Roanoke Island near the present-day city of Manteo . . ."

Boone stared through the windshield with a look of concern. We hadn't heard from John Masters since he took the exit forty minutes ago.

"OBX is a two-hundred-mile-long string of barrier islands that runs the entire length of North Carolina. It's sometimes called the Graveyard of the Atlantic . . ."

I hoped it didn't turn out to be our graveyard, or Malak's, or Bethany's, or John's.

"Ocracoke Island was home base for the pirate Edward Teach, also known as Blackbeard. He was killed on the island by Lieutenant Robert Maynard in 1718. Maynard cut Blackbeard's head off and put it on the bowsprit of his sloop so the bounty could be collected . . ."

I was kind of interested in this factoid, although I have to say that my taste for blood and gory death had changed over the past week or so.

"Orville and Wilbur Wright made history on a windy beach at Kill Devil Hills near the town of Kitty Hawk in North Carolina on December 17, 1903, when they piloted the first plane ever to fly with an engine."

Croc began to growl. We had come up behind a semi-truck.

Boone dropped back and tapped his Bluetooth.

"Felix?"

"Yeah."

"Turn around. We have the truck. Stop at the hospital and pick up the coach."

❖ ❖ ❖

John Masters had never felt more vulnerable in his life as he pushed the shopping cart across the dark parking lot. He kept his head down. If they were out there, they were watching through night scopes. Trailer Guy would not be scanning the lot for active threats. He'd be hunkered down making a beeline for his trailer, completely unaware that his stocking cap might be in the crosshairs of a sniper scope. The closer he got to the cluster of RVs, the better he felt. If they were going to take a shot, they'd do it in the open. But he still didn't let his guard down. He pushed the cart between two motor coaches and stopped at the beat-up trailer parked behind them. The next part of the ruse could prove to be a little tricky. He grabbed two bags and banged on the trailer door.

Lights came on. He banged again. A few seconds later the door opened, revealing the real trailer guy, who was big, bald, and annoyed in his T-shirt and underpants.

"What the—"

"You won!" John said, handing him two of the grocery bags.

He had never seen this fail. If you smile and hand someone something, they take it. It could be a live grenade and they'd take it. And with their hands full, they couldn't take a swing at you.

"Who are—"

"Proud Wal-Mart employee. And you're our four-bag winner!"

"At four o'clock in the—"

"Four at Four we call it. Rain or shine every morning we pick one of our parking lot guests and give them four bags of groceries. I'll grab the other two bags. I'm getting kind of wet out here. All I have to do is get some information from you so you can get back to sleep."

All I have to do is get inside your trailer so the terrorists think I live here and they don't try to kill me.

"I guess that'd be okay."

John grabbed the two remaining bags and jumped into the trailer before Trailer Guy woke up enough to change his mind. He closed the door behind him and set the bags on the kitchen table.

"Be with you in a second," the real trailer guy said as he disappeared into a room in the back.

The trailer was a lot better looking on the inside than it was on the outside. It was clean and well organized. All John had to do now was to stay inside long enough to convince the terrorists that he belonged there.

The man came back out wearing a pair of jeans. "Is this for real?"

"Absolutely," John said. "Usually we don't wake people up. We just leave the groceries outside with a note, but because of the rain my boss thought it would be best to knock."

"I'm not sure it was a good idea or not, but thanks . . . I guess. Kind of weird you picking the groceries out for someone you don't know."

John grinned. "I hear you. The receipt's in one of the bags. You're welcome to exchange what's in there for anything you want. It's over a hundred bucks worth of stuff. The only thing I have to do is . . ." He started checking his pockets. "Dang I left the form back at the store."

"What form?"

"It's just your name, address, and phone number. I'll run over and get it and come back."

"No offense, but how about if I write the information down on a piece of paper so I can go back to sleep."

"Sure. That'll work."

The man scratched the information down and handed it to him. John looked the information over. If terrorists were watching, he'd been inside plenty of time to convince them he wasn't a threat.

"You're a lifesaver, Mr. Timmons," he said, and stepped outside into the rain.

He followed the same path he had taken to the store, scooping up his kit on the way. Before getting into his SUV, he checked it for tampering. It was clean. He booted up the computer and turned on the tracking software. The Tahoe was 1.6 miles away, traveling east on 64, which meant they'd been watching him when he left Wal-Mart and they had made a mistake. They had neglected to check their vehicle for tampering.

Now I'm watching you.

❖ ❖ ❖

Croc had stopped growling. He was sitting up in the backseat, staring through the windshield at the taillights of the semi-truck we were following, like they were juicy rabbits. Angela had stopped her OBX travelogue and had her head poked between the front seats again.

"What if it's not the right truck?" she asked.

It was a good question. There were no markings on the back of the truck and we hadn't seen the side.

"It's the right truck," Boone said.

I wasn't feeling the itch, and Angela definitely wasn't

feeling it. I doubted she had ever felt itchy.

"How old is Croc?" she asked out of the blue.

What did this have to do with anything?

"In dog years?" Boone asked.

"There is no such thing as dog years," Angela said. "They're just years. Dogs simply don't live as long as people. Someone didn't like the idea of dogs dying after a few short years so they came up with the one human year equals seven dog years. Dogs have a median age of twelve point eight years."

Only Angela would know something like this. But why was she bringing the subject up?

"Croc is older than twelve point eight years," Boone said. "How much older I can't say."

"Can't or won't?" Angela asked.

There was an edge of frustration to her question, and I was beginning to see where she was coming from. When it came to personal questions (not that "how old is your dog" is a personal question), Boone was usually annoyingly obtuse. At least I think that's the word. He either answered with some kind of riddle, or chose not to answer at all. This time he decided not to answer at all. He stared through the windshield as if he hadn't heard the question.

My mom and Speed were both surprised that Boone was still alive. He was an old guy when they were young. Mom had also been surprised that Croc was still with him. She thought he must be Croc version 2.0 or 3.0, because the original Croc could not possibly still be alive in human or dog years.

"How old are you?" I asked.

Boone tried to grin the questions off. "Two against one?"

"How old is Croc?" Angela repeated. No grin.

"We're both older than we look." Grin.

"That's not exactly an answer," I said. No grin.

"It might be the best you're going to get right now." Grin. Two frowns.

Boone's grin disappeared. He stared through the windshield. We waited.

"I don't know how old I am," he finally said. "I don't know how old Croc is. But I can tell you this. We are older than anyone you have ever met, or ever will meet. When you're gone, we'll still be here like we've always been here."

I looked at Angela. Her mouth was hanging open and I'm sure mine was too. Boone was not talking about dog years here. He was talking about something entirely different. Something impossible.

"Are you saying you're a vampire?" I asked.

"No," Boone answered. "We killed the last vampire a hundred years ago."

We? I had been joking, but I don't think he was.

"I know it's hard to wrap your mind around the idea," Boone continued. "When this is all over, I'll try to explain it in more detail."

More detail? He hadn't given us *any* detail at all. If anyone but Boone had told me he and his dog were eternal, immortal, or whatever he was saying, I would have thought he was kidding, lying, or crazy. But this was Tyrone Boone. The guy who always seemed to show up in the right place at the right time. The guy who appeared to live on nothing but water and never seemed to sleep. The guy who the president of the United States was trusting with the life of his daughter. The guy who everyone was surprised was still alive.

"Ageless," Angela said quietly.

I was surprised she seemed to be buying into this so easily. She was usually more skeptical than me.

"Something like that," Boone said. "And there's something else you need to know."

"As if what you just told us isn't enough for us to know," I said.

Angela cracked a smile.

Boone actually laughed, then said, "Here's the deal. By this time in a mission, Croc and I are usually pretty much on our own, meaning that we separate from the SOS team and operate out of their view."

"Why?" Angela asked.

"Let's just say that the team doesn't know about some of my special talents. It would freak them out, just like it will freak you out if you happen to see something . . ." He hesitated. "*Impossible* I guess you'd call it. I didn't expect to have you with me. My plan was to pass you off to one of the other team members, but since I'm . . ." He hesitated again.

"Stuck with us," I said.

"I wouldn't put it like that. But I'll admit having you with me could be a little awkward. If down the road I do something a little unusual, I need your word that you won't tell anyone about it, including the other members of the SOS team."

"What do you mean by *unusual?*" I asked.

"Kind of like magic," Boone said.

I looked at Croc. He was sitting up and appeared to be listening to everything we said, and I had a feeling he *understood* what we were saying. It creeped me out and made me feel bad. I'd said some things to him over the past week that weren't exactly kind. I probably wouldn't have said them if I thought he understood what I was saying. And then there were his startling appearances, like when he was on the other side of the overpass and a second later he was at my side.

"Croc seems to move pretty fast at times," I said.

Boone gave me a curious look, then nodded. "He's pretty spry for his age . . . at times."

"What are you talking about?" Angela asked.

Apparently she hadn't seen him do this. I hadn't actually *seen* him do it either. He didn't move from one place to another. He simply appeared.

"He moves fast," I said, which was lame, but I didn't know how else to explain it. One thing I *did* know. I was going to pay a lot more attention to Croc from now on. I was going to keep a closer eye on Boone as well.

"I'm not saying with certainty that you're going to see anything," Boone said. "But if you do, I need your word that you'll keep it to yourself. We've been over this before, but I have to ask: Will you trust me?"

I looked at Angela. "The president does. Malak does."

After a pause, she said, "Fine. I trust you and I won't say anything."

Boone glanced over at me. "And you?"

"My lips are sealed, but I do have one more question." Actually I had a thousand questions, but I didn't think he'd answer them because they had to do with magic. Magicians never reveal the secrets to their tricks.

"You want to know how old the SOS crew is," Boone said.

"That wasn't what I was going to ask, but now that you mention it."

"X-Ray and Vanessa are the oldest of the bunch. They're in their mid-seventies."

"But you're older," Angela said.

"That's right."

"And Croc is older too," I added.

"Much older."

Boone's cell chimed. It was John Masters.

"Saved by the bell," I said.

Boone smiled.

Memorial

John told us about his Wal-Mart terrorist encounter.

"No doubt about it," he ended. "They're pros. Taking them out is not going to be easy."

"The woman you saw is definitely not Malak Turner," Boone said. "And just to clarify, our primary mission is not to take them out. If we eliminated them, four more would pop up. We're after the guy moving the pawns and his lieutenants. No player, no game."

"Understood," John said.

"I'm going to bring everyone into the conversation. X-Ray will link the Tahoe you're tracking to our computers. He'll hack into the Wal-Mart surveillance tapes and try to get some intel on the four bad guys. If they're pros, they're bound to be in a database somewhere. Hang on while I patch them in."

A moment later X-Ray came on the line, complaining how boring it was following a bomb.

"Until it goes off," Uly added.

"They're heading south now," Vanessa said.

Boone ignored the banter and told them what was happening on our end. Within seconds X-Ray had the Tahoe John was following on Angela's computer and added Felix's cell signal so we could track him as well.

"We're only a half a mile behind John," Angela said. "John's a quarter of a mile behind the Tahoe. Felix is just about at the hospital."

"I have a feeling we're all headed to the same place," Boone said. "The Wal-Mart stop wasn't just a supply stop. They were waiting for the truck to catch up."

Ziv checked in, saying their Tahoe had reached its destination.

"Where?"

"The U.S.S. Cole Memorial."

"What's that?" I asked.

Of course Know-It-All knew the answer. "In October 2000, terrorists detonated a boat filled with explosives next to the U.S.S. Cole, which was refueling in a Yemeni port. Seventeen sailors were killed and thirty-nine were wounded."

"Is there a bomb in the car?" Boone asked.

"Yes," Ziv said. "The wires run from the engine to the back of the vehicle. Beneath the carpet is enough plastic explosives to blow up another ship."

"What's around the memorial?"

"Water. A parking lot. A jogging path. Essentially nothing. They parked next to the memorial, then got into an empty car waiting for them in the parking lot. Eben dropped me off here and followed them. They checked into a hotel. He checked their new car. No explosives."

"Are you there, Eben?" Boone asked.

"In the Rover watching the hotel," Eben said.

"Let them go. They aren't important. X-Ray? See if there is anything scheduled for the Cole Memorial today."

X-Ray came on a minute later. "Nothing that I can find."

"Then it's symbolic," Boone said. "As long as we can do it without any collateral damage, we'll let the Tahoe explode. They can erect another memorial. Felix blew the first bomb prematurely. We'll do this one early too. Hopefully they'll conclude it was faulty timers, not outside interference. X-Ray will walk you through the procedure for resetting the timer."

"Go ahead, Ziv," Eben said. "I'll pick you up after you have it done."

"Very humorous," Ziv said.

Several people laughed. Boone didn't.

"After the Tahoe goes up," he said, "get down here as soon as you can. He hasn't said it, but I don't think it will be too long before J.R. sends the troops in to get his daughter back. I can't blame him. If he does, and Malak doesn't have the head ghost in hand, this will all be for nothing. The ghost cell will go dark. We need options. If the head ghost isn't at the other end, we need a way to keep Malak in the game. We may need to bring back our rogue Mossad agent."

"Providing the rogue Mossad agent survives the blast," Eben said.

"Best be careful," Boone said.

◇◇◇

Felix pulled into the hospital parking lot wishing he could climb inside the coach and go to sleep for about three and a half days. He also wished there were some clothes inside that weren't singed and torn that would fit him. But he knew fresh clothes and a long sleep were not on the agenda.

At least I'll be able to get something to eat.

Then he remembered that Roger and Blaze were vegetarians and there wasn't anything inside that he would want to put into his mouth. His only hope was that Q had a secret cache of eatable food he could raid. He would have gotten something at the Cracker Barrel, but thought better of it when he saw his reflection in the window of the restaurant. He looked like a grizzly bear that had been caught in a terrible forest fire, or a very large man who had fallen on a live grenade and somehow survived. He felt it would be best if he stayed out of sight until he got himself cleaned up. He had found a pink cell phone in an old Ford Taurus with plenty of battery left. He didn't mind the color, but the constant buzzing of incoming calls was annoying. Whoever owned it was popular, or else they were calling their own phone trying to find out where it was. He'd thought about heisting the Taurus, but it didn't look roadworthy. Instead he decided on the Benz, but not before switching license plates with the Taurus to confuse the cops.

He parked next to the coach and got out. The weather had improved. It was still raining, but not nearly as hard as it had been. The wind had died down to about fifteen miles an hour. He stretched. His whole body felt brittle as if it might shatter if he fell down or bumped into something. He would have liked to get right into the coach and take off, but Boone wanted him to find out what had happened to Q's dad.

Out of sight, out of mind and good riddance to him, Felix thought. *What's he doing down here anyway?*

But Felix knew Boone wouldn't have asked him to check unless he thought it was important, so he trudged across the wet parking lot to the entrance and walked inside. The woman behind the desk looked surprised. Then alarmed, as Felix got closer.

"May I help you?" she asked nervously.

Felix looked at the name tag on her scrubs. Her name was Betty.

"I'm looking for Speed Paulsen."

She gave him a fake smile and checked her computer terminal. "I'm afraid we don't have a Paulsen as a patient here."

"He's not a patient. He was visiting."

Two uniformed security men hurried around the corner.

Felix glanced at them. They split up and flanked him. One to the right, one to the left.

Here we go.

"We don't give out information about our visitors, or our patients," Betty said.

The security guards moved in on him. Felix reached into his tattered coat and pulled out his wallet and flipped it open.

"Federal agent," he said. "Stand down."

The security guards stopped in their tracks. The one on his right looked at his creds. Felix moved the badge so Betty could read it. The badge read: "Special Agent Felix Park,

Homeland Security." If they were to call in to check the creds, they would find that Felix Park was an active agent of the federal government currently assigned to Homeland Security, compliments of the magic-hacking fingers of Raymond Brock. Felix also had creds for the Federal Bureau of Investigation, National Security Agency, Department of Defense, and the Central Intelligence Agency. The SOS team all carried a pocketful of creds.

"What in the world would Homeland Security want with Speed Paulsen?" Betty asked.

"We don't give out information about our fugitives, or perpetrators."

Felix was beginning to enjoy himself now, a little. "Where is he?"

"He was here, but he left," Betty said. "It was a little confusing, really. He came in with his son, then his son disappeared, then he asked about some patients that were in a truck accident, but we didn't have any record of them ever being here. Then his car wouldn't start."

"We managed to get it going," one of the security guards said. The name on his badge was Ralph. "Then he took off. Said he was heading down to the Florida Keys."

"What about his alleged son?"

"I don't know what all that was about," Betty answered. "He was concerned when we couldn't find him, but he seemed to forget the whole thing after a while. He couldn't have been nicer. He signed autographs and talked to everyone."

"Weird night," Ralph said. "While we were trying to get Speed's car started, one of the doctors discovered that his car had been stolen."

"Thanks for the information."

"What happened to you?" Ralph asked.

"What do you mean?"

"Your clothes. You look like you've been beat up."

"You look like you were set on fire," the other guard said.

"That's classified."

Felix walked out of the hospital and back to the coach. He fumbled around in the wheel well for the magnetic lockbox with the spare key. It wasn't exactly where Boone said it would be, but he finally found it.

He stepped inside the coach and fired up the diesel engine. While it was warming up, he checked out Q's bunk for food and was rewarded with a half a bag of stale potato chips and a candy bar with a bite out of it.

Better than nothing.

The candy bar was gone by the time he got back to the driver's seat. He buckled in, put the chip bag between his legs, and booted up the dashboard computer. Boone and Masters were almost to the town of Manteo on Roanoke Island. The intellimobile was a couple of hundred miles away, heading south on I-85 toward Atlanta. Ziv and Eben were getting ready to set a car bomb off. He was glad he wasn't with them. He'd had enough of car bombs for one day.

Boom

Eben stood at the back of the Tahoe with a flashlight in one hand and a cell phone in the other. Ziv was standing next to him, holding a screwdriver and a pair of wire cutters. Everyone was listening in, but X-Ray was the only one giving instructions. Ziv had just gently peeled back the carpet in the cargo area. Beneath it were several pounds of C-4 plastic explosives. Dozens of stainless steel balls had been embedded into the soft plastic to increase the damage. There was a digital timer clicking off the minutes, one second at a time. It was set to go off in a little less than three hours.

"You sure it takes both of us?" Eben asked.

"Yeah," X-Ray said. "One to hold the camera phone so I can see what you're doing, and one to disarm the bomb."

"I hate bombs," Eben said.

"It's a lot of explosive for a little memorial," X-Ray said, ignoring him. "This might have been their secondary target."

"Can we just get this over with," Ziv said impatiently.

"Sure," X-Ray said. "Cut the blue wire."

"Just like that?" Ziv said.

"Snip," X-Ray said. "But cut it up toward the lead because you're going to need to reattach it. You'll need some slack to reach."

"Why don't I just disconnect it from the lead?" Ziv asked.

"Because the bomb would explode," X-Ray said.

Ziv pointed to what he thought was the blue wire.

Eben leaned down with the flashlight for a closer look. "Blue."

Ziv cut it. Both men closed their eyes as if this would help if the Tahoe exploded. It didn't explode.

"Show me the timer again."

Eben pointed the camera phone at the timer. The numbers had stopped.

"Perfect," X-Ray said. "Now detach the green wire. Don't cut it. Just pull it away from the contact. Gently."

"So this one we don't cut," Ziv said.

"Weird, isn't it? Detonators all have their little quirks. You cut this one and the bomb goes boom."

Ziv pulled the wire off the lead. Gently.

"Set the countdown timer for five minutes."

"Five minutes!" Eben said.

"Any longer and a jogger or someone might show up. You heard Boone. He doesn't want any collateral damage. Five minutes should give you plenty of time to get out of the blast radius."

"Our vehicle is two hundred feet away in the parking lot," Ziv said.

"You'll have to run."

Ziv looked at Eben. "Make sure you have your keys out, ready to go."

Eben nodded. "I hope the car starts."

Ziv set the timer for five minutes.

"Okay," X-Ray said. "Hook the green wire up again. Gently."

Ziv reattached the green wire to the lead.

"Now the blue wire. You'll have to expose the end and hook it to the lead as best as you can, but make sure it's secure. If it pops off. Boom."

Ziv took out a small knife and exposed the copper on the wire.

"This is the tricky part. The timer is going to start the moment it touches the lead. And remember to make sure you don't lose contact or—"

"We know," Ziv said. "Boom."

"Exactly."

Ziv looked at Eben. Sweat ran down both of their faces. "Ready?"

"Do it," Eben said.

Ziv wrapped the wire around the contact.

04:59 . . . 04:58 . . . 04:57 . . .

"Run!" Ziv shouted.

Eben was the first to reach the Range Rover.

04:23 . . .

He jumped in and started the engine.

04:19 . . .

Ziv dove into the passenger seat and slammed the door.

04:13 . . .

Eben put the Rover into gear but kept his foot on the brake. "Do you see anyone coming?"

They looked up and down the road for headlights and people.

"I don't see anyone," Ziv said.

04:01 . . .

"Shall we go?" Ziv said. "There is a leopard waiting for us down south."

Eben stepped on the gas and peeled out of the parking lot. He decided that if he saw an approaching car, he would swerve into it to stop it. There was nothing he could do if a car came up behind him.

Ziv stared down at his watch. "Two minutes give or take a few seconds."

Eben rounded a curve, relieved to see no oncoming cars and hoping none were coming up behind them.

"Forty-five seconds."

They were two point five miles away when they heard the boom.

Bridges

"Listen," Malak said.

"I don't hear anything," Bethany said.

"The clicking sound. Every four seconds or so. Here it comes."

Click …

"What is it?"

"The tires running over something across the road at regular intervals. I think we're on a bridge. A long bridge. We must be going over a body of water. I don't know this part of the country very well."

"Lucky for us I do," Bethany said. "I virtually lived on buses through two long presidential campaigns. You think we turned west of I-95?"

"I'm pretty sure."

"How long ago?"

"Two hours."

"Then we're on Highway 64. We're crossing the bridge to Roanoke Island. If we cross another bridge after this, we'll be on the Outer Banks."

"You're certain?"

"As certain as a blind person can be about where they are. But I can't think of any other long bridges in this part of the country."

"Blind person," Malak said. "Brilliant."

"What are you talking about?" Bethany asked.

"I'm going to find out what else they have in this truck. I'll have to do it by feel."

"I'll help you."

"No. You need to stay where you are. You're supposed to be unconscious. We can't risk them stopping and finding you out of place. I'll be back."

Bethany laughed. "Where else are you going to go?"

"Good point."

Ten feet from the back doors was a heavy curtain of plastic suspended from the ceiling hanging all the way to the floor. Malak had noticed it when they got into the truck, but had thought nothing of it. She'd assumed it was there to keep the cool air from escaping when the doors were opened. She had also assumed that the truck was empty. That she and Bethany were the only cargo. She crawled under the plastic and discovered that she was wrong. The curtain was concealing something quite large. But what?

She crawled along the right side of the trailer trying to make sense of what it was by nothing more than touch. The bottom part was made out of square metal tubing. It felt like a frame of some kind. It was strapped down with webbed cinch straps as tight as bowstrings. She crawled farther along and came across a different texture. It was rubbery, pliant. Beneath the rubber she felt metal again, with small protuberances sticking out from it.

Lug nuts. It's a tire.

She felt farther along and came to another tire.

It's not a car. The tires are too close together.

The truck slowed. She braced herself and listened. The clicking had stopped. She stood and put her hands out. She felt something smooth, almost slick. It wasn't metal.

What is this thing?

She stretched her hands above her head, following the smooth surface upward until she felt an edge sticking out a foot or so above her head. It was rougher than the other surface. It was rounded on the side and flat on the top. It felt like wood. And suddenly she knew what she was touching.

A gunwale. This is a boat. A good-sized boat.

The truck was moving steadily, but it had definitely slowed. Now that she knew what it was she debated going back and joining Bethany, but thought better of it. The best way to defend yourself against the cell was to know things about them they didn't think you knew. They wouldn't be hauling a boat unless they planned to use it. She hooked her fingers over the gunwale and pulled herself up, wishing she had paid better attention to all the boats she'd been in during her life. It was on a trailer so the bow had to be pointing toward the doors.

Maybe.

She hadn't followed the boat for its entire length. There was a chance they had pulled it straight into the trailer and the vehicle was still attached. One thing was certain, it was too big to have been pushed, or pulled, into the trailer by hand. She crawled to her right until she bumped into what felt like steps. There were four of them. They led to a door. She fumbled for the handle, opened it, stood, and stepped through. She felt the wheel. To the right of the wheel were several knobs and levers and . . .

A key.

She turned it one notch. Instrument lights came on, dimly, but enough for her to see her surroundings. There was a flashlight bolted to the wall. She grabbed it and turned it on. She wasn't sure what she was searching for. She started opening cupboards, then she heard the clicking again.

Click . . . click . . . click . . .

They were passing over the second bridge.

Poof!

"Drop back," Boone said. "Get a visual on the truck to confirm, then pull in several cars behind us. That way we can hopscotch with the truck down the road."

"Roger that," John said.

We had just crossed Roanoke Island, bypassing Manteo, and were rolling onto the Washington Baum bridge toward the Outer Banks. The truck was several car lengths ahead of us, but it was easy to see in the distance because it was the only truck on the road.

A couple minutes later John called back. "Maryland Fish Company," he said. "Big red crab on the side. The Tahoe and the truck are heading north on 158."

Boone's cell buzzed the second he ended the call with John. It was the president.

"Just got word of a car bomb obliterating the Cole Memorial," J.R. said. "You know anything about that?"

"Yep," Boone said, then explained why he had allowed the car bomb to go off.

"It was a good decision. They're reporting no casualties. The same can't be said for another explosion on I-95. They're telling me there were at least two fatalities."

"When they finally pick up all the pieces, they're going to find out there were four fatalities. They were all bad guys."

"Any more car bombs?"

"Probably, but we're on them."

"And my daughter?"

"She's right in front of us."

"Any idea when I can have her back?"

"I can have her free in five minutes if that's what you want," Boone said. "She's your daughter. It's totally up to you."

He didn't mention that we had lost Bethany for several hours during the night.

"You think she's safe?" the president said.

"No, I don't," Boone said. "None of us is safe as long as the ghost cell is operational. But I do think Malak will do everything she can to protect her."

After a long pause, J.R. said, "I moved the SEAL team to Norfolk."

"I thought you might," Boone said.

"The weather's flyable. They can be where you are in less than an hour."

"We might need them yet. I'll let you know."

Boone ended the call.

John came back on again. "I'm behind you. Maybe twenty cars back. What's with all this traffic?"

He was right. There were a lot of cars and they were

barely moving. The road was flat and straight and stretched for miles. There were cars for as far as we could see. Red and blue emergency lights flashed in the distance. The traffic came to a complete stop.

"This is going to make them nervous," Boone said.

"Is it a roadblock?" Angela asked.

"Don't think so," Boone said. "If it was a roadblock, we'd have oncoming traffic. They'd be letting cars through after checking them. It must be an accident or maybe a road problem."

People started opening their doors and getting out of their cars. Boone rolled his window down. A guy walked by and Boone asked him what was going on.

"Power pole went down up ahead. I have a buddy closer to where it happened. Cops say it'll be at least twenty minutes before they get it cleared up."

"Why's there so much traffic?"

"Commuters. No work in OBX unless you want to clean hotel rooms or sling hash in a restaurant. We work in Norfolk. Hour and a half on a good day each way. This isn't a good day."

"I guess not," Boone said. "Is there a way around the jam?"

"You could cut through the residential area and get ahead of it, but it'd be a hassle. There are a lot of dead ends. I'm a local and I don't know how to do it. Most of us just wait it out here, or turn around and find someplace to get coffee."

It looked like a lot of people were choosing the coffee option by jockeying their cars out of line and turning around.

"Thanks for the info," Boone said.

The man wandered off. Boone undid his seat belt.

"Where are you going?" Angela asked.

"I'm going to check some things out. I'll be back soon. You two stay here."

Croc squeezed between the seats and joined him outside on the road. I glanced at Angela. When I looked back, Boone and Croc were gone. I looked out to the front, back, and sides. There was no sign of them.

Angela was craning her neck looking for them too. "Where'd they go?"

I jumped out of the Audi. Angela joined me.

"There!" She was pointing up the road.

It was dark, but in the headlights we could just make out a guy and his dog walking up the empty left-hand lane. They were at least a hundred and fifty yards away, well beyond the crab truck and probably the Tahoe as well. An Olympic sprinter could not have covered that much distance in the seconds it had taken them to get where they were.

"Impossible," Angela said.

"Poof," I said.

"I'm serious, Q."

"So am I." I told her about Croc's *impossible* move on the overpass.

"Why didn't you tell me this before?"

"This is the first time we've been alone," I said. "And you wouldn't have believed me anyway."

"Probably not," Angela admitted.

Boone and Croc were now too far away for us to see.

"Where do you think they're going?" I asked.

Angela didn't answer. She had turned her attention to the truck, which was about seventy-five yards in front of us.

"I'm not sure which is weirder," she said. "Boone and Croc teleporting, or whatever you want to call it, or knowing my mom and the president's daughter are in the back of that truck."

For me it wasn't even close. Boone and Croc hands down.

But why had they only gone a hundred and fifty yards? If they could teleport, why not go directly to where they wanted to go? Maybe there was a limit to how far they could travel. Or maybe they had ended up exactly where they wanted to be before switching to walking mode. I wondered if he could teach me to . . .

"Then there's that whole ageless thing," Angela said, interrupting my busy mind. "That has to go on the weird list. What do you think of–"

Angela was interrupted by a man and a woman holding guns to our heads.

The man yanked our arms behind our backs, zipped flex-cuffs around our wrists, and had us into the backseat of the Audi within seconds. No chance to run. No chance for Angela to kick him in the head. No chance to call for help. Not that anyone would have heard us. Two cars behind us and the one in front had bugged out for coffee, or to find a way around the jam.

"Search them," the woman said. "If they resist, shoot them."

We didn't resist. The man tossed Angela's backpack to the woman, then he proceeded to pull everything we had out of our pockets. Angela's pockets were pretty easy. All she had was her cell phone. He showed it to the woman.

"I'll be back in a minute," she said, taking it.

My pockets were a little more of a challenge for the man. I had six large pockets in my cargo pants. He pulled out four decks of cards, three lengths of rope, silk hankies, seven magic coins, flashlight, camera, sunglasses, baseball cap, *Goldfinger* by Ian Fleming (paperback), a Leatherman tool, and a stack of "special" dollar bills.

"How about leaving me one deck of cards," I said.

"How about if I break your neck?"

"Keep the cards," I said.

He stuffed everything into a plastic bag, tossed it off into the dark, then climbed into the driver's seat and slammed the door. The woman returned, minus Angela's pack and cell phone, and got into the passenger seat. She was tall. Her black hair was pulled back in a severe ponytail. It had to be the same woman John had run into in Wal-Mart. T3 he called her.

"Hot wired," the man said, pointing at the wires dangling from the transmission.

The woman nodded, turned to us, and pointed her gun at Angela. "Where's the old man?"

"You mean our grandfather?" Angela asked.

The woman cocked the pistol. "It would be best not to lie to me."

"He's walking his dog," I said.

"We'll continue this conversation in a few minutes. Someplace more private."

"I think you're mistaking us for someone else," Angela said.

"I don't make mistakes." The woman turned to the man. "Get us out of here."

The man fiddled with the dangling wires. The engine started.

Now would be a good time for Boone and Croc to reappear and scare the living daylights out of them. Or for John Masters to show up and shoot them.

But no one came.

The man backed the Audi out of the traffic, hung a U-turn, and took a side street to someplace more private.

Poof! We're gone.

Blink

Boone stood at the roadblock with all the other bystanders and watched the road crew clear away the debris from the power pole. The highway was ten minutes from opening up. He called John as he started back and told him to track his cell signal.

"I'm already tracking it," John said. "You just walked up to the head of the traffic jam. How long before we start moving?"

"Shouldn't be too long, but that's the least of our problems."

"What's up?"

"Just let me know when I'm even with the Tahoe."

"A white Chevy Tahoe shouldn't be too hard to see for yourself," John said. "Even in the dark."

"Humor me," Boone said. "Is Angela's cell signal stationary?"

"Yep. It's exactly where it was when you went for your walk. There was a little glitch with your signal. It kind of shot ahead for a moment, then settled down."

"Yeah, it does that," Boone said, thinking that he needed

to be more careful with his signal. "I guess I need to get a better phone. Let me know about the Tahoe."

Seven minutes later John let him know.

There wasn't a white Chevy Tahoe within two hundred feet in either direction from where Boone was standing. The closest vehicle to him was a red truck. Boone walked over to talk to the driver. A middle-aged man drinking coffee from a thermos cup lowered the window.

Boone squatted down so they could talk face-to-face. "Did you see a white SUV in line?"

"Yeah. There was one parked right in front of me. A gal got out of it and asked what was going on. Tall. Pretty. Squatted down like you. Told her about the power pole. She got back in and they did a U-turn." He pointed to a side street. "Looking for a way around I guess."

"How long ago?" Boone ran his hand under the door frame.

"Twenty minutes. Maybe a bit longer."

"How many were in the car?" Boone found what he was looking for.

"I don't know. Looked like four of them. Are you a cop?" The man laughed. "Well . . . an ex-cop?"

Boone smiled. "No. They're friends of mine. I walked up here to say hello and was surprised they were gone. I better get back to my car before the traffic starts moving."

He walked away, flipping the switch on the device he had found under the man's door frame. His cell phone buzzed.

"The Tahoe just went off-line," John said.

"The Tahoe isn't here," Boone said. "They found the

tracker and stuck it on another car."

"When?"

"Half hour ago or so, so they're not too far away. But they're onto us. And that's a big problem. Hang on . . . X-Ray is calling in."

"I've taken a look at the Wal-Mart video," X-Ray said. "We've got four really bad guys . . . Correction. Three really bad guys and one really bad girl. Like Masters thought, they are definitely a team. They've been all over the world blowing things up and killing people for a variety of terrorist groups. The woman has more aliases than I have fingers and toes, and if you connect the dots, there's a good chance that she not only knows the Leopard, but they've worked together. Masters was also right about who's in charge. It's T3 all the way. I ran a program on their micro-expressions. The three tough guys are actually afraid of her."

"Keep data mining and let me know what else you come up with."

Boone bent down and gave Croc a scratch on the head. "Time to move, partner." He looked around to see if anyone was watching, then blinked himself back to the Audi.

When they materialized, Croc started growling, but there was nothing to growl at. The Audi wasn't there.

Boone swore.

Croc walked over to Angela's phone, picked it up, dropped it next to Boone's cowboy boots, then trotted away again.

Boone picked up the phone and put it in his pocket.

I shouldn't have left them alone. Mistake.

His cell phone buzzed. It was John.

"Your tracking signal had that weird glitch again."

"We have bigger problems. The Audi's gone and so are the kids."

Boone heard John's car fire up. "I'll be right there."

Less than a minute later, John's black SUV came roaring up the left lane and screeched to a stop next to him. He got out.

"A lot of cars have turned around and driven by me," he said. "But the Audi wasn't one of them."

"Then they took a side road," Boone said. "There were several of them in front and behind them."

"What do you want to do?"

What Boone wanted to do was call in J.R.'s SEAL team and tell them to take out every terrorist within a hundred miles, but he knew from long experience that wasn't the answer. Not yet anyway. T3 and her crew were told to take Q and Angela. He didn't think they would have acted on their own. And there was a decent chance that they had waited until he went for his little walk. He wondered if they had seen him *blink*. That's what he had always called it because of the speed at which it happened. He doubted they had seen it. If they had, they probably would have waited for him to come back. He looked down the road at the truck. He wished he could blink himself inside and talk to Malak, but it didn't work that way. He could blink himself anywhere, but not through solid matter. If he was inside something and wanted to leave, he had to use an opening like everyone else.

"We'll stick with the truck," Boone said. "For the time being anyway. I don't think they'll hurt Angela and Q until they know exactly what's going on. They're running security on the truck and they're not going to stray too far from it. And when Malak sees they have Q and Angela, she's certainly not going to let anything happen to them."

"Those kids must be scared out of their minds," John said.

"I wouldn't count on it. After what they've been through the past couple weeks, they don't scare too easily. They know what's at stake here."

"This your dog?" John asked.

Boone looked down. Croc was sitting at his feet with five playing cards in his mouth. "Yeah," he said. Boone took the cards from him and fanned them out. It was the ace through the ten of hearts.

"Royal flush, huh. Winning hand. We'll see."

John was staring at him and Croc.

"The cards belong to Q," Boone said by way of explanation. He could see from John's expression that it wasn't good enough.

"His name's Croc," he said. "He's a little quirky."

His phone buzzed. It was the president.

"I'm tracking Q and Angela's signals and it doesn't appear they're with you," J.R. said.

The Seamaster watches. He'd forgotten they were wearing them. The terrorists hadn't taken everything. Boone had his Seamaster in the coach. He didn't want the president tracking his every move, but he was obviously tracking his cell phone signal. How else would he know that Angela and Q weren't with him? He wondered what he had thought of the blink.

"That's right," Boone said. "They're not with us at the

moment. Don't have time to give you more details than that. Can you transfer their signals over to John's rig? I'm riding with him."

"Shouldn't be a problem. Is everything okay, Boone?"

"Better now. You know how things go at this stage of the game. Everything's fluid. Talk to you soon." He looked at John. The traffic had started to move. "Let's go."

John climbed into the driver's seat. Boone walked around the SUV and squatted down so John couldn't see him. He reached into his pocket and came out with the tracking device he'd taken from the red truck.

"Go find them," he whispered into Croc's ear. "Stick this back on the Tahoe. And don't worry about Angela and Q seeing you blink. They're onto us. But the terrorists aren't. It would be best if they didn't catch that trick."

Croc gently took the tracking device into his mouth and vanished.

Boone climbed in next to John. J.R. had been right. The years had been kind to John Masters. He looked alert and very fit. "It's good to see you again, John."

"You too." John gave him a curious look. "You haven't changed."

"Oh, I'm a lot older than the last time we met, and I'm feeling it right now, but thanks."

"We have two new blips on the screen."

"That would be Q and Angela. They're both wearing Seamasters."

John looked at his watch. "He can track us with these things?"

Boone nodded. "He likes to know where his friends are."

"Where's your dog?" John asked as he started to crawl forward with the other cars.

"He's around," Boone said. "He'll find us down the road. He always does."

T3

We pulled up behind a white Chevy Tahoe with two guys standing next to it. I wondered if there was a bomb inside.

T3 looked at us from the front seat. "I'll be back in a minute," she said. "And when I get back, you better have the right answers."

She and the driver got out to talk to the two other terrorists.

"Did they take your watch?" Angela asked.

"I'm not sure. My hands are asleep."

"Let me see."

I turned around so she could see my wrists.

"It's there," she said.

Hers was there too.

"At least the president will be able to find our bodies," I said.

"I don't think they're going to kill us," Angela said. "At least not yet. Let me handle the questioning."

"Why?"

"Because I'm a better liar than you."

She had me there. She *was* a better liar than me, but I was improving.

"You should have seen me lying to my dad," I said. "It would have blown you away."

"I'm sure," Angela said. "Any chance you can get out of your cuffs?"

"I'm working on it."

I had flexed my wrists when he ratcheted them down. There was some play in them, but not enough to get my hands free. Yet. The trick was to take your time and not fight the cuffs. If you start yanking and struggling, your wrists swell and the cuffs get tighter. And getting out of them was only half the problem. I'd still have to figure out a way to get Angela out of hers. Without something to cut them with, that wasn't going to be easy.

"Another thing," Angela said. "We need to act more afraid."

"I don't know about you," I said. "But I am terrified."

"I am too," she said. "But we're not acting terrified."

"You want me to start shivering, or pee my pants?"

"No, but I think we need to start acting like two kids who have no idea why they've been abducted and are afraid they might be murdered."

"That shouldn't be too hard since we don't know why they've taken us, and T3 seems more than willing to kill us."

"You know what I mean," Angela said.

"Yeah, yeah, I know what you mean. But I'd skip the 'Boone is our grandfather' story. That's not working." I looked out the window. T3 and the driver were on their way back to us. "Get ready to act scared."

T3 opened the back door on my side and pointed her gun at me. I smashed myself up against Angela as if that would somehow save me from a bullet.

"Let's start again," T3 said. "And this time I hope you get it right because if you don't, one of you is going to die right here, right now. Who are you?"

"My name is Angela Tucker," Angela said, her voice quaking and her lips trembling. She looked pretty scared to me. "This is my stepbrother, Quest Munoz."

I wanted to correct her over the Quest thing, but that probably wasn't what someone who was ready to pee his pants would say.

"Finally we have a little truth," T3 said. "But we already knew what your names were. We also know who your parents are and that you were at their concert last night in the White House."

This was information, or intel as Boone would call it, that anyone who could read could get off the Internet. It didn't mean there was another mole in the White House feeding them information.

"What I want to know is, who is Tyrone Boone? Why is he following us? Who else is with him? Why did he put a tracking device on our car when we were inside the store?"

This was great news. If she thought Boone had placed the tracking device on their car at Wal-Mart, then she didn't know about John Masters.

"Boone is our parents' driver," Angela said shakily. And it was pretty convincing. "He's also in charge of tour security. He's been acting kind of strange lately. Paranoid. He was supposed to be driving us to our parents' concert date in San Antonio. On the way there, he said the guys driving the equipment truck were in an accident. We stopped by the hospital to see if they were okay, then Boone showed up in this car and drove us out this way. When we asked him why, he said that he had uncovered a plot to kidnap us. I guess he knew you were after us."

A look of confusion crossed T3's face. I tried to hide my own confusion. Where was Angela going with this?

"Why did you tell me that Tyrone was your grandfather?"

"It just slipped out. I didn't know who you were. We still don't know!"

That was pretty lame, but T3 let it go.

"What about the tracking device?" she asked.

"I don't know anything about it," the petrified Angela said, talking fast like you would if you were scared to death. "I don't even know what it is. Boone stopped at a Wal-Mart . . . well, about a block away from a Wal-Mart. He told us he had to do something, and for us to wait in the car. We talked about getting away from him, but we didn't know where we were, or where to go. He wasn't gone for more than ten minutes."

"Was he looking at a GPS?"

"He was looking at his phone, but he's always looking at his phone, even when he drives. It could be a GPS."

"What about your motor coach?" T3 asked. "What about the stolen car?"

Oops. She obviously knew a lot more about us and the situation than she was saying. There had to be someone else feeding her information, because they hadn't been anywhere near the hospital when Boone had jacked the car. The only explanation could be that they had a countersurveillance team out there that we didn't know about. It was lucky they hadn't spotted John Masters. And it could be that the reason they didn't spot him was that they were watching us.

"Boone said the coach had broken down," Angela said in a rush. "He said he had borrowed the car from someone at the hospital. We didn't know it was stolen until your driver pointed it out!" She literally shrieked this last part out, which I thought was a nice touch.

T3 wasn't nearly as fond of the screech as I was. She lunged forward and hit me in the face. It was shocking and it hurt, but the pain was lessened by my automatic reflex to defend myself. My hands were still behind my back, but they were free of the flex-cuff.

"Keep you voice down," T3 said.

"I didn't say anything," I said. I felt warm blood running out my nose.

"Here's how it works," T3 said. "If one does something to annoy me, the other gets punished."

She backed out and slammed the door.

"Are you okay?" Angela asked.

"Next time I'll do the talking and *you* take the punishment," I said, then wiped my nose.

"Your hands!" Angela said.

"Pretty cool, huh?"

"Don't let them see."

I'd been watching them the whole time. They were talking to each other outside the Tahoe, paying absolutely no attention to us.

"Keep an eye on them." I tilted my head back and pinched my nostrils closed.

"Can you free my hands?"

I slipped my left hand behind her back. There was absolutely no play in her flex-cuff.

"Have you been trying to get yourself free?" I asked, which probably sounded pretty weird with my nose pinched shut.

"Yes," Angela answered.

"Well, stop," I said, releasing my nose. The pinch seemed to have done the trick. "Your wrists are swollen. You're making it worse. Any chance you can do tae kwon do with your hands tied behind your back?"

Angela shook her head. "I don't think so."

We looked out the window. The terrorists had turned toward us and were lit up by the headlights of the Tahoe. That's when I saw Croc appear. He materialized three feet behind them right next to the SUV. One of the terrorists must have heard something. He turned his head, but by the time his eyes got there, Croc was gone.

"Poof," Angela said.

"You saw it?"

"I wouldn't have believed it if I hadn't. Do you think Boone is with him?"

"I didn't see him."

"Where do you think they go when they vanish?"

"I'm not sure they vanish," I said.

"What do you mean? We just saw Croc vanish."

"I'm not exactly sure what we saw," I said. "I know a lot about tricks and illusions. Smoke and mirror stuff. But this is way beyond me. I think if you disappear, you have to appear someplace else. I don't think they vanish. I think they move from one place to another faster than we can see."

"And you know this how?"

"I don't really know it. I'm guessing. The terrorist that turned felt something. Or maybe he smelled something. I don't know if you've noticed, but Croc has some personal hygiene issues."

"He stinks," Angela said.

"Exactly, but I wouldn't say that in front of him. It might hurt his feelings. He can't communicate with us beyond barking, growling, belching, and farting, but I think he understands everything we say."

"I've said some terrible things in front of him."

"Me too," I said. "I think Croc not only moves fast, he can see fast. I bet this applies to Boone as well, otherwise people would have been onto him years ago. It's like the old Superman comics where Clark Kent goes into a phone booth to put on his blue Spandex and cape faster than the eye can see. Croc's probably been off in the shadows watching for a while. He must have waited for them to turn and look in our direction before he made his final move."

"But we saw Boone disappear, or move, on the highway."

"We saw him move because he wanted us to see him move. He showed us what he was capable of so when we saw it down the road we wouldn't completely freak out."

"I'm pretty freaked out," Angela said.

"Me too, but I'm getting used to the idea."

"Croc showed himself so we'd know he was here," Angela said.

I was hoping that when this was all over, Boone could *show me* how to move like this. If a dog could do it, why couldn't I? But I didn't mention this to Angela.

"I think that's exactly what Croc did," I said.

T3 got into the Tahoe with two of the other men. The fourth terrorist walked over to the Audi. I put my hands behind my back, hoping that he wasn't going to shoot us in the backseat. It would be just my luck to be murdered before I got a chance to talk to Boone about his and Croc's *unusual abilities*. It was the same guy that had driven us here. He opened the driver's door and slid in.

"I don't want to hear a word out of either one of you," he said without looking at us, and started the engine.

I wasn't interested in talking to him anyway. He pulled in behind the Tahoe and headed north on back roads. The sky was lightening. Angela and I kept our eyes glued to our windows. Croc appeared twice on my side and three times on Angela's side. It was good to know he was with us.

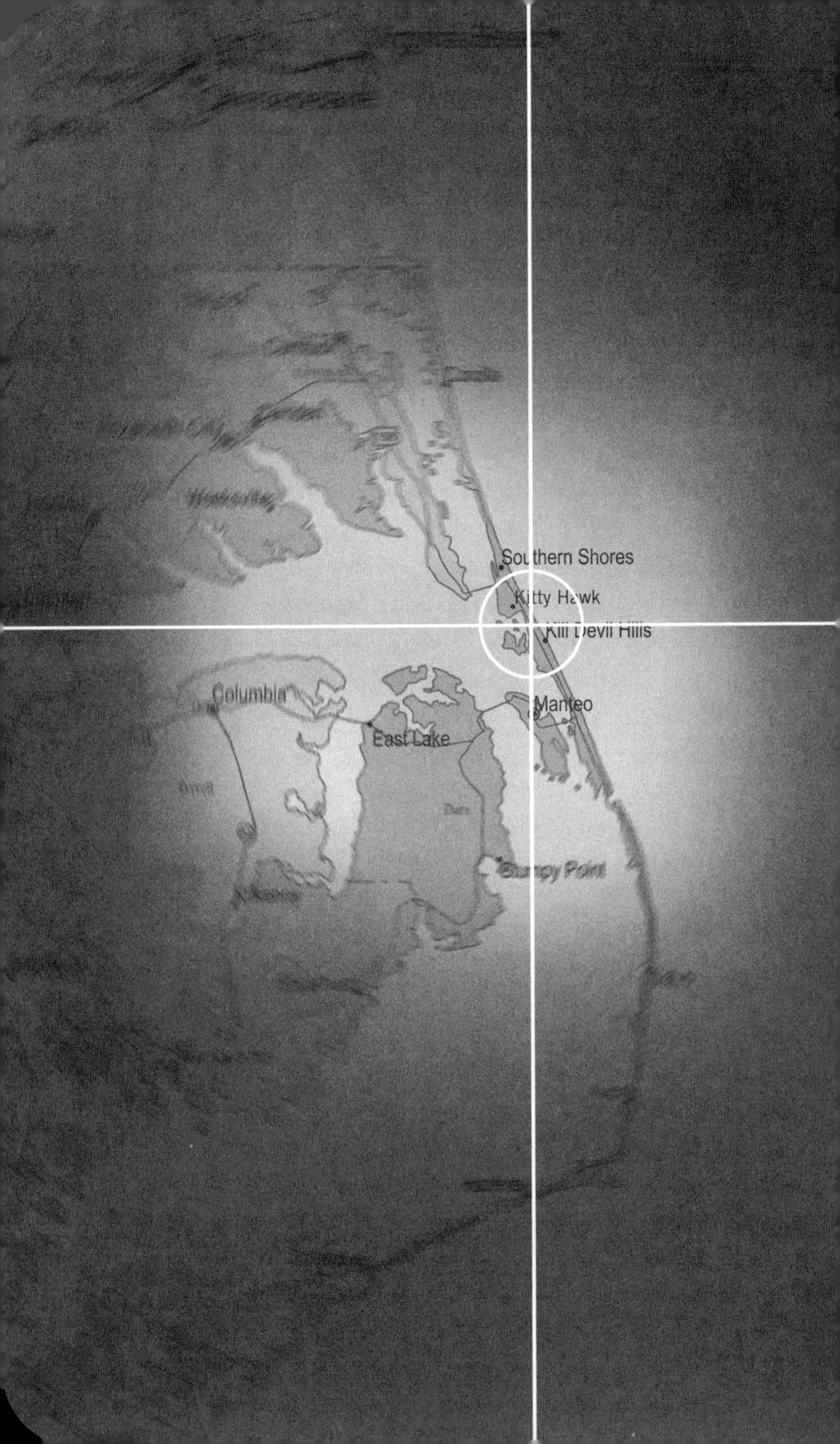
Southern Shores
Kitty Hawk
Kill Devil Hills
Columbia
Manteo
East Lake
Stumpy Point

SUNDAY, SEPTEMBER 7 >

6:45 a.m. to 9:15 a.m.

Kitty Hawk

The sun was coming up. It looked like it was going to be a clear day on the Outer Banks.

Boone watched the dashboard computer in John's SUV. Another signal had appeared on the GPS a few minutes earlier. It had been a little hard to explain to John how this had happened, so Boone had simply told him the truth, or a version of the truth.

"Croc put the tracking devise back on the Tahoe."

"Your dog?"

"Yep."

"Wow. That's a good dog," John had said, and dropped the subject.

It was then that Boone knew he and John were going to get along well.

The Tahoe and the Audi were driving parallel to them about a half a mile inland along Bay Drive. Eben and Ziv were barreling south on 158 and were about a half an hour out. Felix was just crossing the bridge to Roanoke Island.

"Turn signal," John said.

Boone looked through the windshield. The truck was turning left onto Kitty Hawk Boulevard.

"Back off," Boone said. "Give them plenty of room." He pointed to the GPS. "The Tahoe and the other vehicle are going to intersect with the truck a half a mile down."

Boone called the president.

"Looks like it's going down in Kitty Hawk," J.R. said.

"Maybe," Boone said. "Might be time to move your team in a little closer just in case."

"I already have," J.R. said.

Boone wasn't surprised. "Where are they?"

"South of you. First Flight Airport. Kill Devil Hills. They landed about twenty minutes ago."

"How many?"

"Eight operators. Half a platoon."

Boone thought for a minute before responding. "Do you think there'd be any objection to Masters taking the lead on this?"

"I'm the commander in chief," J.R. said. "The SEAL team will do what I order them to do."

"Putting that aside," Boone said.

"I don't think there will be any objection. These boys would be thrilled to take orders from John Masters."

"Let them know," Boone said. "He'll be down at Kill Devil Hills soon. This needs to look like an Israeli Mossad operation. No American involvement."

"Understood," J.R. said.

"This is my last call until this is over."

"Get her back, Boone," J.R. said, and ended the call.

Boone called Eben and Ziv next. Ziv answered. "Go to the First Flight Airport in Kill Devil Hills and suit up. Make certain you're wearing vests. Your lives will depend on it. The Mossad is going to do an illegal favor for the president of the United States."

"I have great admiration for your Culpepper president," Ziv said. "It will be my pleasure to do a favor for him."

The last call Boone made was to Felix.

"How are you holding up?"

"Tired," Felix said. "Sore."

"You can take your time getting here. I think we have enough people. We'll need you to pick us up later this morning."

"I'll get breakfast," Felix said. "There's an outlet mall up ahead. Big and Tall shop. I need new clothes."

"I'm not sure where we'll resurface," Boone said. "I'll give you a call when I know."

Boone turned to John. "Stop the car."

"The truck's getting quite a ways in front of us," John said.

"Pull over."

John pulled into a gas station.

"I'm getting out here," Boone said.

"Why?"

"End game," Boone answered. "You probably caught some of the conversation, but there's a SEAL team waiting for you at the First Flight Airport. You'll be in command. It's strictly black op. Way off the books. I'll give you more instructions when you get there."

"The Tahoe and Audi are now heading south on Elijah Baum Road. The truck's probably with them. They're a mile away. How are you going to get there?"

"Don't worry about it. I'll catch up with them. Get going. You'll need to be in place soon."

"Are you sure about this?"

"Yep."

John pulled his pistol out of the holder and offered it to him. Boone smiled and shook his head. "Weapons are your deal," he said, getting out. "I won't need it."

He watched John pull a U-turn. As soon as John was out of sight, he turned his cell phone off.

Then he blinked.

Dead Kids Tell No Tales

It seemed like they had been in the truck for weeks. Malak looked at her watch. 6:53. They had been in the truck for less than four hours. She switched on the flashlight she had found in the boat and shined it at Bethany. Other than looking a little rumpled and tired, the president's daughter appeared to be in remarkably good shape. She even managed to give Malak a slight smile.

"So this is it," Bethany said.

"I suspect so. Are we clear on everything?"

"My part's pretty simple," Bethany said. "Play dead."

"Unconscious," Malak corrected. "There's a stretcher in the boat."

"I sometimes get a little queasy on boats. Do you know how far we're going?"

There had been a nautical map in the boat with a course plotted to a small island in Kitty Hawk Bay.

"It's not far," Malak said.

She handed Bethany the hood. "Sorry."

"That's all right," Bethany said. She slipped it on, lay down, and began her deep yoga breathing.

The truck came to a stop.

Malak went into a state the polar opposite of Bethany's. Every nerve in her body was on high alert. She pulled out her pistol, chambered a round, and pointed it at the door. To protect Bethany, and to protect herself, she needed to bound from the truck like a leopard ready to hunt. She needed to be completely in charge.

The locking mechanism screeched. A moment later the doors swung open. Light poured in. The Leopard did not shade her eyes. They were parked in the middle of a cemetery. The white Tahoe was backed up to the rear of the semi-trailer. Exhaust billowed out of the mufflers in the cool morning, past the tombstones. Three men surrounded it, facing out, assault rifles ready. Scuff Boots started pulling out the ramp. A woman stood to the side of the open door. She was tall, with long black hair pulled back into a severe ponytail. Malak knew her as Ariel, aka the Lion of God. She had a cell phone to her ear with one hand, and an assault rifle in the other.

Malak lowered her pistol, but kept it in her hand. She had worked with Ariel several times before. She and her team's specialty was security and assassinations.

"The hostage is alive?" Ariel asked.

Malak nodded, wondering if Ariel knew who the hostage was. There was a good chance she didn't. She was high up in the cell, but several notches beneath Anmar the Leopard. She got down from the truck.

"Alive," Ariel said into the phone, then handed the phone

to Malak. "For you."

"Congratulations," a man said. "You are now officially one of the Five."

It was the same man who had questioned her in Virginia, but she only knew his voice. He hadn't allowed her to see his face. Hopefully that would now change. He had told her that if she succeeded in kidnapping Bethany Culpepper, she would become a member of the inner circle. If she failed, he would have her killed. She glanced at Ariel. There was no doubt in her mind who her assassin would have been. She had not heard of *the Five* before. The name implied there was more than one person in charge of the ghost cell. This was the worst possible news she could have received. It meant that her journey would not end today.

"Bethany is well?" the man asked.

"She's still unconscious, but stable," Malak said. "She was overdosed."

"She will wake soon. There is a map in the boat. Bring her to me. Ariel will set up a security perimeter around us. The only people allowed inside will be you, Bethany, and the other two. We try to keep our identities secret. I will tell Ariel that you are in charge of the operation, but I will not tell her that you are one of the Five."

"The other two?" Malak asked, thinking they must be members of the Five she hadn't seen yet.

"The children," the man said. "Angela Tucker and Quest Munoz."

It was all Malak could do to stop her knees from buckling. "They're here? Why?"

"It was voted upon," the man said. "I will explain how the Five works when we get a chance. You'll find it interesting. Put Ariel on the phone. I'm looking forward to finally meeting you face-to-face."

Malak handed Ariel the phone, keeping her face completely neutral although she wanted to scream. Ariel listened, then handed the phone back. Her face was neutral as well, but Malak was certain she wasn't happy to hear that the Leopard was in charge of the Lion.

"I assume Tyrone Boone was with the children," Malak said.

"He was driving," Ariel said. "But he wasn't there when we made the snatch. We didn't take him."

"He couldn't have been too far away. Why didn't you wait for him to come back?"

"We were led to believe he wasn't an important asset. Our primary mission was to make sure the truck arrived here without any interference. The children were a target of opportunity. We were told to take whoever we could and not to harm them. There was no time to search the highway for the old man. There was a traffic jam. Many people were out of their cars. Too many witnesses."

Ariel had made a huge mistake in not apprehending Boone, but Malak didn't ask any more questions. To do so would tip her hand. Ariel could not know the Leopard was in the dark.

"Where are the children?" Malak asked.

"Around the corner in a car."

"I'll go speak with them."

"I already questioned them," Ariel said. "The girl lies badly."

"I'll see if I can get some truth out of her," Malak said. "I want you to supervise the loading of our cargo. Use the stretcher from the boat. Handle her gently. I don't want her woken until we are ready for her. And this is not the place. I assume the truck will haul the cars away from here?"

Ariel nodded. "We leave no trails."

Malak nodded. Another one of the ghost cell mottos.

"See to it. I'll get the children out of the other car so you can move it. I'll bring them over when the boat is loaded and ready to leave. It's best they see and hear as little as possible."

Ariel smiled and shrugged. "It doesn't matter," she said. "Dead kids tell no tales."

Malak returned the smile, but she was sick with dread.

Dead terrorists tell no tales either.

She walked around the side of the truck to the second car . . . and her daughter.

A Voice from the Grave

"Here comes your mom," I said.

"I see her," Angela said.

"She doesn't look too happy." Actually she looked furious. She was walking quickly toward us with her gun out.

"I imagine not. She just rode half the night in the back of a semi-truck after kidnapping the president's daughter. Now she's in the middle of a graveyard, and we're here."

"That'd be enough to tick anybody off," I said. "But I'm glad to see her anyway. It means we may not die today."

Malak yanked the door open. She looked even angrier close-up.

"Get out of the car!"

I knew it was an act, but it still scared me. T3 seemed nice in comparison. We got out.

She pointed. "Walk over to that bench and sit down."

There was a stone bench about a hundred feet away surrounded by tombstones. We walked over to it and sat down with our backs to the truck. She came up behind us and quickly cut our flex-cuffs . . . well, Angela's cuffs. Mine were already off. She squatted in front of us so the people at the truck couldn't see her. Only then did she give us a small worried smile.

"I can't say that I'm happy to see you here, but I am happy to see that you're both alive."

Tears ran down Angela's cheeks.

"You need to get all of that out of your system right now," Malak said. "When we get in that boat, you need to stop thinking of me as your mother. If anyone suspects our true relationship, we will all be dead. Now tell me what happened, quickly, from the time you left the White House until you got here. We have very little time."

Angela gave her a quick and pretty concise summary of what had happened, skipping a few points, like Croc sniffing out their whereabouts in the crab truck and his and Boone's ability to vanish into thin air, or teleport, or whatever they did.

When she finished, Malak looked at me. "So your dad followed you from D.C.?"

"Yeah. He's not wrapped too tight. But it kind of worked out for us in the end."

"And they don't know about this John Masters guy?"

"I don't think so," Angela answered. "They thought Boone put the tracking device on their car."

"Do you have any idea where Boone and Masters are?"

"I'm here," Boone said to our right.

"Don't look!" Malak warned us.

Angela and I stared straight ahead.

"I'm not impressed with your idea of protecting my

daughter," Malak said, staring at us.

"We can discuss that at another time," Boone said.

"I assume your team is here?"

"No," Boone said. "Just me."

A look of anger and disappointment crossed Malak's face. Of course she didn't know about Boone's special talents.

"Are you armed?" Malak asked.

"Nope."

"That's just perfect."

"Who were you talking to on the phone?" Boone said.

"How long have you been here?"

"I got here before you arrived."

"How did you know—"

"There's no time to explain," Boone said, cutting her off. "Who were you talking to?"

"The same man I talked to in Virginia. He's on an island waiting for us. The cell is controlled by five people. He's just one of them."

"So if we get him, we still have four more to go," Boone said.

"Three," Malak said. "I'm one of the five now."

"That's good to hear," Boone said. "We need to keep you in that five so we can take the rest of them down."

"How?"

"The Mossad is going to do a raid on the island led by the rogue agents Eben and Ziv. They're going to rescue Bethany Culpepper and return her to the president. The guy waiting for you on the island is going to be wounded. But not too badly. You're going to save him by shooting Eben and Ziv.

They'll have their vests on. Shoot them in the chest. No head shots. After they're "dead," you're going to get away to fight another day."

"There's a woman here named Ariel. She'll be setting up a parameter with three pros. They're not going to be easy to take out."

"I suspect the Navy SEAL team posing as Israeli Mossad will be up to the challenge," Boone said.

"What about intel from the island?" Malak said. "The team will need to know what they're up against. I have a phone now, but I can't risk using it. They might be tracking outgoing data."

"No worries," Boone said. "Q will be providing intel for us."

"I will?"

"Sleight of hand," Boone said. "I've seen how you can conceal a phone in your hand to snap photos. This time you're going to use video. You'll need to get interior room shots, doors, approaches to the house. It'd be nice to get a shot of where Ariel sets up her team. Just think about what kind of information you would need if you were going to storm the island with an assault team. Make sure you don't get caught doing it. And you won't have much time. As soon as they get you in the house, or whatever they have out there, they're going to lock you and Angela in a room. As soon as you're alone, upload the video to John. We'll be along not too long after we get the video. If you can't manage to get the shots, we'll still be along, but not quite as efficiently."

"You're forgetting something," I said.

"What's that?"

"I don't have a phone."

"Angela's phone is under the bench right next to your feet. I've programmed John's number into it."

"It takes a long time to upload video," I said. "And there's a size limit."

"It will upload instantly," Boone said. "And there's no size limit on Angela's phone. X-Ray has messed with it."

"Ariel's coming," Malak said.

She was halfway between us and the bench, moving quickly.

I picked up Angela's phone. Croc had been messing with it too. It was covered in dog drool.

The Hunt

Before we got into the boat, Ariel wanted to put flex-cuffs back on us, which would have killed the video idea. I'm pretty good, but I didn't think I could manage a camera phone with my hands cinched behind my back.

"Once the cuffs were off, the girl told me some interesting things," Malak said. "And I don't think she was lying."

"Such as?" Ariel asked.

Malak answered her question with another question. "What can they do to us? They're children."

There were a lot of things Angela could do now that her hands were free, but the question had its desired effect. Ariel climbed into the boat and shut up about it.

The boat was made out of aluminum and it was good-sized. The enclosed cabin was long enough to hold the stretcher. Malak gave the coordinates to one of the men. She told Ariel to take the bow and put the other two men on the starboard and port sides. Malak, Angela, and I sat in the stern. This allowed me to practice with the phone without anyone seeing, and for Angela and her mom to talk quietly without anyone hearing. I tried not to listen, but it was kind of hard not to. We were sitting three feet away from each other.

"So what's going to happen?" Angela asked.

"Violence," Malak said. "Boone's team is going to move in and surgically take out Ariel's team. Then they'll storm the house. You and Q will be locked in a room and won't hear much. The SEAL team will probably use silenced weapons."

"That's not what I meant," Angela said. "What I want to know is what's going to happen to you?"

"Oh," Malak said, a little startled. "I'll be fine. Since Ariel won't be around to defend herself, I'll put the blame for the raid on her. I suspect that whoever gave her the order will do the same. They should have never taken you without taking Boone. You and Q obviously didn't put the tracking device on their SUV. They had the president's daughter in hand and one of the five had the bright idea to break protocol and kidnap you. It was a stupid mistake. The ghost cell has not survived all of these years by making mistakes. I might be able to cause some dissension among the four. Maybe I can get them to take out one of their own."

"And then there were three," Angela said.

Malak smiled. "I hope it gets to, *And Then There Were None*."

"You mean *one*," Angela said.

"Definitely," Malak said. "Remember the Agatha Christie novels we read together when you were young."

"I remember," Angela said. "I remember all of the books we read together."

"I thought this was going to be over today," Malak said.

"I can see now that was wishful thinking. But I am closer to being done with this than I was a few days ago."

"What are you going to do when it's finally over?"

"I try not to think about that too much. Thoughts like that are dangerous for me. I suppose I could move back to San Francisco. I've always loved the city. I'd have to change my identity of course. I think I'd like to become a librarian."

"You're kidding."

"No joke. I love books, and believe it or not, I like helping people."

"That's hard to picture," Angela said. "I mean, the librarian part."

It was impossible for me to picture too. Malak didn't look like any of the librarians I'd ever known.

She gave Angela a wistful smile. "Sometimes at night when I'm trying to sleep, I imagine myself walking down an endless aisle of books, running my fingers along the spines, pausing once in a while to pull a book off the shelf to see what's beneath the cover. I know it's kind of an odd fantasy for an infamous international terrorist."

"You're not a terrorist," Angela said.

"Actually, I am a terrorist," Malak said sadly. "I have done some very terrible things. Things that I deeply regret, but I had little choice if I wanted to stay in the hunt." She looked off across the water for a moment, and bit her lower lip just like Angela did sometimes. When she looked back, there were tears in her eyes. "It's been all about the hunt," she said softly. "It's why I went off the grid. It's why I stepped into Anmar's shoes. It's why I lied to your father. It's why I lied to you."

"You didn't lie," Angela insisted.

"Yes I did. Letting your loved ones think that you are dead is a lie. I broke your father's heart. I broke your heart. All for the hunt."

"Someone had to do it," Angela said.

"But I volunteered," Malak said. "You and your father didn't. I brought you both into this. Now I need to get you out of it."

"We all need to get out of this," Angela said. "Including you."

"That may not be possible. There are a lot of people looking for me and they aren't going to stop just because I decide to stop hunting. If we're lucky enough to take the ghost cell down, there will be more people looking for me. We won't get all of them. There will be some that are too deeply buried for us to dig out. It will only take one of them to kill the librarian in the stacks. If they find out you're my daughter, they'll come after you too. They'll come after your father as well. These people are vindictive and they have long memories. It's a deadly game I'm playing. And to be truthful, I'm not sure how to end it."

"I think it can be worked out," Angela said.

"We'll see. I hope you're right. But first we have to get through this day."

"Boone's plan seems pretty good," Angela said.

"Boone's plan is absolutely brilliant, but don't tell him I said that. I'm still ticked off at him for leaving you and Q alone on the highway." Malak stood up. "I better check on Bethany."

"Is she okay?" I asked, thinking it might be all right for me to butt in now. "She's been unconscious for a long time."

"She's as conscious as you are," Malak said. "She woke up at the rest area. She's doing something called deep yoga breathing to make everyone think that she's out. That girl has more grit than her dad, and that's saying something. The point of this exercise is to video the president's daughter, striking terror into everyone's hearts. We're not going to give them that chance."

She went into the cabin.

"What do you think?" Angela asked.

"I think your mom's pretty cool. I think she's right about your and her situation being complicated. I think I'm going to be able to get the video Boone needs, but I don't think it was necessary."

"What do you mean?"

"I think Boone and Croc are already on the island and know exactly what the setup is there."

"If he's already there, why doesn't he just shoot the video and send it to John?"

"Because he doesn't want to turn his cell phone on. It's being tracked. How can he explain traveling over open water at the speed of light? Remember when he turned his cell phone off in D.C.?"

Angela nodded.

"I thought he did it because he wanted to be off the grid, but that wasn't it. He turned his cell off so he wouldn't have to explain how his signal went from point A to point B in a millisecond."

"Who do you think Tyrone Boone really is?"

"A better question might be *what* is Tyrone Boone? And the answer is, I don't know. I'm just glad he's on our side."

Malak came back a few minutes later and sat down next to us. "We'll be there in about five minutes. I just got a call from the man on the island. This is how it's going to go down. We'll carry Bethany up to the house on the stretcher and put her in the room to the right. You two will be going into the room to the left. Ariel and her team will exit the house and set up their perimeter outside. When everyone is gone, the man will make his appearance."

"He doesn't want anyone to see what he looks like except you," Angela said.

"Exactly," Malak said, looking at me. "The point is that you might not have a lot of time to get the video Boone needs. I'll have Ariel's team take the stretcher, and we'll follow behind, which should give you a chance to get some shots. But even though they're in front, you'll need to be careful. The man will be watching us closely as we approach the house."

"He won't see the camera," I said.

The boat started to slow. Fifty feet in front of us was a long dock.

"The actual raid will happen very quickly," Malak said. "By quickly I mean it will be over within a minute or two. Bethany is the president's daughter. They'll treat her as if the threat is still active, even if the bad guys are all dead. Their immediate priority will be to get her off the island to a secure location. With some luck, I'll be gone before she leaves." She looked at Angela and hesitated. "What I'm saying is this is it. I love you. Stay away from the doors and windows when the shooting starts. I'll be in touch when I think it's safe. Tell Boone thanks, but I'm still mad at him."

We were ten feet from the dock.

"I hope the hunt ends soon," Angela said.

"I do too," Malak said.

The House

"Tie up with the bow facing the bay," Malak said. "We may have to get out of here quickly."

The man on the bridge swung the boat around and eased it into the dock next to a second boat that was smaller than ours, but looked a lot faster.

Ariel and another man jumped to the dock and fixed the lines fore and aft to cleats. It was a nice dock. It looked like it was made out of solid teak or some other expensive wood.

Ariel pointed at a couple of her men and told them to take the stretcher.

"Negative," Malak said. "I want one person on each corner."

"It's not that heavy," Ariel said.

"That's not the point," Malak snapped. "I don't want her jostled. I don't want her awake until we have her inside." She looked at each terrorist in turn. "Do you understand?"

They all nodded, but it was pretty clear they didn't like Malak ordering them around.

"What about the kids?" Ariel asked.

"I can handle two kids," Malak said. "We'll be right behind you. Let's go."

We waited in the boat until they had the stretcher out and had started up the dock.

"Let's go," Malak said to us, waving her gun for the benefit of anyone who might be watching. I was shoulder to shoulder with Angela. Malak was two steps behind us. I started the camera rolling, moving it to the left and right, but mostly focusing the tiny lens on the house. The house was a two-story log A-frame set back into the trees about fifty feet from the dock. A set of steep stairs led up to a porch that ran the length of the house. It looked like the front door was wide open. I figured the guy would be upstairs looking out the window but standing back a ways so nobody could see him. Malak hadn't mentioned it, but I also figured that he had binoculars or a spotting scope. I would have in his place. This meant he could see us like we were standing a foot away from him.

A magic trick is all about diversion. You get them to look at your left hand so they don't see what you're doing with your right hand. How was I going to keep this guy's attention off my right hand, where I had the phone? Simple. I started picking my nose with my left hand. It's a perfect diversion. People have two fundamental reactions to nose picking. They are either so grossed out they can't look at you at all, or they are kind of fascinated by the process and can't take their eyes off of it, especially if they think you can't see them. If they're nose-picking lookers I guarantee they're not watching the hand that isn't digging. And I had a lot to dig because of the bloody nose Ariel had given me.

Apparently Angela was not a looker. She glanced at me once, saw my busy index finger, and didn't look at me again all the way into the house.

The house was magnificent. It looked like they'd knocked down an entire old-growth forest to build it. Inside, it was nicely furnished and it smelled like pine. Stuffed animal heads were sticking out of the log walls. Polar bear, moose, lion, wildebeest, rhino, and several animals I didn't recognize. On the floor were zebra-skin and tiger-skin rugs. Directly across from the front door was a wide staircase leading up to an open balcony running all the way around the top of the A. There were rooms on the front side of the house and on the back side. I figured the guy that was watching us was in one of the upstairs rooms in the front. I also figured that he didn't own this place and probably had no connection to it whatsoever. No one would kidnap the president's daughter and take her to his own house.

Malak pointed to the door on the far right of the lower level. "Take her in there," she said. "Lay the stretcher on the bed."

She gave me another second to video the interior of the house, then she pushed us toward an open doorway on the left side of the house. As soon as we were inside, she slammed the door behind us.

Croc was stretched out on the king-sized bed with his brown eye open and his blue eye closed.

Even though I had predicted he was going to get to the island before us, I was shocked to see him.

Angela looked shocked too, but she stayed on task. "The video," she said.

"Right."

There wasn't time to see if what I'd shot was any good. I attached the file to an e-mail to John and hit the send button. Within a second the e-mail was gone.

"That was fast," I said.

"Where do you think Boone is?" Angela asked.

"Close by."

I checked out the walk-in closet, then went into the attached bathroom. I didn't expect to find Boone that close by, but I had to look. The bathroom window was open. I looked out. It was at least a fifteen-foot drop to the ground in back. If Croc had come through the window, he would have had to have flown. There were bushes and trees in back of the house. A lot of places for Navy SEALs to sneak up on terrorists without being seen. One of the terrorists came around the corner and took up a position behind a tree. He wasn't paying any attention to the house, so I shot a short video of him and sent it to John with a note telling him where I had taken it.

When I came back out, Angela was sitting on the edge of the bed scratching Croc's ears. She was crying. I sat down next to her, wondering if I should give her a hug, or take her hand, or put my arm around her. I wasn't clear on what new stepbrothers should do in a situation like this. I ran back into the bathroom and grabbed the box of tissues. I handed it to her. She gave me a little smile, pulled a tissue out, and wiped her eyes.

"Thanks, Q."

"Sure. I know this thing with your mom is really hard."

"I'll be okay. It's just that I thought it was going to be over today."

"I did too."

She went into the bathroom. I could hear the faucet come on.

I walked over to the window. I wanted to see if the terrorist was in the same spot. He was. And that's when I saw Boone. He appeared right behind the guy, held up three fingers to the window, then he was gone. The guy turned his head, but of course there was nothing for him to see.

Angela came out of the bathroom.

"I just saw Boone."

"Where?"

"Out back. We have three minutes."

Three Minutes

Malak watched out the front window as Ariel settled into her position at the front of the house. Four sides to a house. Four positions. It was a logical configuration and one that Boone's team would have no problem anticipating. She went into Bethany's bedroom, leaned close to her ear, and whispered, "This will be over soon. Do not move."

"How is she doing?" a deep voice asked behind her.

She had expected him, but had not heard him approach. *He moves like a ghost.* He had waited for Ariel to show up out front before coming out of hiding. She turned to face him.

He was standing in the doorway. He was shorter than she thought he would be. Five foot eight. He had black hair graying at the temples. He was wearing pressed jeans, a gray sweatshirt, and deck shoes without socks. He was lean, but not thin. He was fit for a man in his mid-fifties. But the most important thing she noticed about him was that he was not armed. He did not look like a terrorist, but people in the ghost cell rarely did. He looked like what he was supposed to be. A successful businessman spending the weekend at his extravagant man lodge in Kitty Hawk Bay.

"She will be fine," Malak said. "I think she'll be awake in two or three hours."

"Excellent." He stepped into the room. "That will give us time to talk, but before we do, please remove the hood. I want to see her face, and she will probably be able to breath easier with it off."

Malak knew the man was not interested in Bethany's comfort. He wanted proof that it was the president's daughter lying on the bed. She gently removed the hood, hoping Bethany could continue her yoga breathing under this kind of scrutiny.

The man walked over to the bed and stared down at her for several seconds. Bethany's breathing was deep and regular, making Malak wonder if she actually was asleep or unconscious.

"She is a beautiful young woman," the man finally said. "We will let her sleep. Let's go talk. I'm sure you have many questions for me."

She followed him into the big room, closing Bethany's door behind her with a huge sense of relief.

So far so good.

"Can I get you anything?" the man asked. "I can make coffee or tea. You must be hungry after your uncomfortable journey, but I'm afraid there isn't much to eat in the kitchen. Did you bring supplies?"

"In the boat," Malak said. "I'll go down to get them in a moment."

The man smiled. "Talk before eating. Of course. Please sit down."

She sat facing the window trying to anticipate how the raid would go down, wondering how soon it would happen. She needed to be in position. She needed to be close to the man regardless of when it happened. He sat down in a chair directly across from her, not four feet away.

"Interesting house," she said.

"A hunter's house. He is currently in Alaska fishing, according to the caretaker, who is one of ours."

"The caretaker is here?"

"Of course not. He is actually driving to Texas in one of the SUVs you saw at the rest area. The owner of the house is not due back for several days. We have someone watching his house on the mainland in case he returns early, which I doubt. And according to our person in Alaska, the owner is having a wonderful time. The fish are biting. But I'm being rude. I haven't introduced myself. My name is Paul Smailes."

"Glad to meet you *face-to-face*," Malak said.

"Ah yes, our meeting in Virginia. A necessary threat, I'm afraid. There were suspicions about you because of Elise and Amun's deaths. Your adopted mother, my sister, my son, all dead in an instant. I am sad they are gone, but life and our mission moves on, does it not? You have certainly proven yourself worthy of the Five."

Time to test the waters. To find out if I'm actually one of the Five.

"What's the caretaker doing in Texas?" Malak asked.

"A car bomb," Paul answered immediately, as if the question didn't bother him in the least. "He's with three others. We haven't quite decided where to place the bomb as of yet, or if we will even detonate it. Now that you are one of the Five, you will be in on that decision."

"Why wouldn't we detonate it?" Malak asked.

"We've had some timer problems. At least that's what we think. Three of the vehicles last night were carrying bombs. Not the vehicle you and Bethany were in, of course. We do not have our best assets drive bombs around." He gave her a small smile. "The car bombs were meant as a diversion to draw police away from the route you were taking down here."

"What happened?"

"One exploded on I-95 killing everyone inside and a pedestrian that had stopped to help them when their car broke down. The second vehicle exploded two hours early. Our target was a naval admiral in Norfolk who jogs along the waterfront every morning at the exact same time. We've been clocking his daily run for months. The time and route never varies. This morning he was to be jogging with a senator on the Armed Services Committee. The bomb was placed at the U.S.S. Cole memorial."

"Fitting," Malak said. "What happened?"

"The bomb went off prematurely, destroying the memorial, but sadly missing our primary targets by several hours."

"Too bad," Malak said. "Maybe we should turn the bomb heading to Texas around and try again."

"That is a possibility, but first we have to have the timer examined. We have someone meeting the Tahoe in Texas. He is very good. If it is faulty, he will be able to repair it. The third vehicle was our roving bomb. We usually have one.

Sometimes we use it, sometimes we don't. We had one in the D.C. bombings. It's still there waiting for a target."

"Smart," Malak said. She would have to find out where it was parked so she could have it disarmed. "When will we decide on the targets?"

"Within a few days. You and I will be traveling to Texas after we finish our business with Bethany Culpepper and the children."

Malak did not react even though he was talking about killing Bethany, Angela, and Q. The ghost cell did not keep hostages for very long. Hostages were used, then disposed of. Keeping them caused too much exposure.

"I wanted to ask you about the children," Malak said calmly.

"Yes. Quest Munoz and Angela Tucker. I understand you know them."

"I *saw* them at the White House. Why were they taken?"

"A target of opportunity."

"Perhaps I'm overstepping my bounds as a new member of the Five, but taking them was stupid."

She watched Paul's reaction to this very carefully. He frowned and nodded. "I voted against it."

"Voted?"

"You'll be meeting the others in Texas, and all of this will be explained in detail. We don't often get together because it's too dangerous for us to be in the same place at the same time. One of the exceptions is when a new member joins the Five. Two of the five were already going to be in Texas, so it seemed the best place to meet."

Malak nodded, relishing the idea of having them all in the same room at the same time.

"Of course Ariel will be running security for us while we're in Texas," he said.

No she won't. She and her team will be dead in a few minutes.

"Of course," Malak said. "Can we get back to why the children were taken and the voting?"

It's time to plant the seeds of sedition among the Five.

"It's simple really," Paul said. "We have five members and each of us has a vote, but the votes are skewed. My position among the five is number four. I have one half vote. You have taken Elise's position at number five. You also have one half vote. Position number three has a full vote. Position number two had two votes. Position number one has three votes."

"So the person in position number one is really in charge," Malak said.

Paul shook his head. "Not really. If you add the votes together there are a total of seven. If number one wants to launch an operation that the other four disagree with, than he loses by four votes to three. There is no lobbying by the other members. The operational ideas are floated completely anonymously. Take the kidnapping of Q and Angela, for instance. It was discovered that Tyrone Boone had placed a tracking device on the Tahoe, and we're following it. Obviously he is not who he appears to be. He needed to be removed. The first idea was to simply have Ariel take him and the children out. That was my idea. I've been watching this Tyrone Boone for several weeks and I believe he's a major player, but I'm not exactly clear what team he is playing for."

It wasn't easy to keep her face neutral as this monster talked so casually about giving the order to have Angela assassinated.

"What happened?"

"The vote was unanimous. Six and a half votes, because you were not yet onboard. But then one of the five added what we call a change order. The children's parents are famous and very popular right now. The idea was floated that we should kidnap the children and video them along with the president's daughter. I voted against this. I thought it was too big of a risk to the current mission. I did not prevail. The vote was two and a half to four. When Boone wasn't in the car, Ariel wanted to leave one of her men behind to wait for him. I voted for that, but again I was voted down."

"For what it's worth," Malak said. "I would have voted with you. I don't know who this Tyrone Boone is, but I don't like the fact that he's . . ."

The front door burst open. Malak's shock and surprise were genuine. She hadn't expected them so soon. Boone must have figured out the destination before they arrived. Eben Lavi was the first through the door. As she pushed Paul down to the floor, she shot Eben in the chest. He flew backward and hit a wall.

"The president's daughter!" Paul shouted.

"No time!" She pulled him to his feet. "There are more of them. We need to get out of here. The boats!"

She dragged him through the front door.

Ziv was waiting for them. He put a bullet in Paul's shoulder. Paul screamed and went down. Malak shot Ziv twice, knocking him off the porch. She yanked Paul back up again.

He grimaced in pain. "Maybe there were only . . ."

The windows on either side of the door shattered in an explosion of glass.

She pulled Paul down the steps. Silenced bullets zipped by their heads. They ran past Ariel, who was slumped forward with her weapon still in her hands, a bullet hole in her head.

"Are your keys in your boat?" Malak shouted.

"Yes," Paul answered, breathlessly clutching his shoulder.

"I'll cut the lines, you start the engine!"

They ran along the dock as bullets splintered the wood around them. Malak pulled her knife and flipped open the blade one-handed. Paul jumped into the boat. Malak cut the lines. The engine roared to life.

"Go! Go! Go!" she shouted, diving over the gunwale.

The boat nearly capsized with the surge of power he had given it. Malak crawled forward and took over the controls. Paul slumped to the deck. Blood oozed between his fingers. His face had gone pale.

"Who were they?" he asked weakly.

"The first man through was Eben Lavi."

"Mossad," Paul said.

Number Five nodded and headed for open water.

Silence

We heard a crash, three shots, two more crashes, then silence.

"Is it over?" Angela asked.

"I don't know. It doesn't seem possible it could be over that quickly. It hasn't been a minute since we heard the first shot."

We were hiding behind the bed staring at the door. If there was going to be trouble, it was going to come through there. Croc was still sprawled out on the expensive bedspread, but both of his eyes were open and his head was up.

The doorknob started to turn. I held my breath. Croc started scratching his ear with his hind foot. I knew we were safe. He would have growled otherwise. Boone opened the door.

"You two okay?"

We stood up.

"That's it?" I asked.

"That's it," Boone said. "These things happen a lot faster than they do in the movies."

"My mother's safe?"

"Yep," Boone said. "She got away. Leopards are hard to catch."

"It happened a lot sooner than I thought it would," I said. "The team was here within two minutes after you arrived."

"And you and Croc were here before us," I said under my breath.

Boone ignored the comment. "Come on out. Someone wants to talk to you before they leave. And they're in a hurry to get her out of here."

We stepped out of the bedroom. Bethany Culpepper was standing in the living room surrounded by two heavily armed men. I recognized John Masters from the video inside his SUV.

"We have a chopper coming in for the evac," he said. "ETA less than a minute."

Bethany looked at us and smiled, then took Angela's hand. "I just want you to know that your mother is the bravest person I've ever met. This country owes her a huge debt of gratitude for her sacrifices, which can never be repaid. If there is anything I can ever do for you . . ." She tapped the watch around Angela's wrist. "I'm ten digits away." She looked at me. "That goes for you too, Q."

The roar of the helicopter came through the shattered windows.

"You coming with us?" John asked Boone.

Boone shook his head. "We have our own ride. I'll call J.R. and tell him you're on your way. Thanks for your help. It was good working with you again."

They shook hands.

"Another chopper is on its way to clean up the mess," one of the SEALs said.

By *mess*, I assumed he meant Ariel and her team. There were two men in front of the house zipping something into a large bag.

John and the other SEAL escorted Bethany out the door to the waiting helicopter. We stepped out onto the porch. Eben was sitting on the steps, looking tired and battered. Sitting next to him was Ziv. We hadn't seen him since Philadelphia, where he was posing as a policeman outside Independence Hall. Angela hadn't seen him since she had discovered that he was her grandfather, which I guess made him my step-grandfather.

"Are you all right?" Boone asked them.

"We will live," Ziv said.

"Next time someone else needs to get shot," Eben said.

"Quit your complaining," Ziv said. "The Leopard shot me twice, and she's my daughter." He looked at Angela. "We have a few minutes before the second helicopter arrives. Perhaps we should go for a walk."

"I'd like that," Angela said quietly.

Ziv got stiffly to his feet.

Bethany climbed into the helicopter. As soon as she was in, it took off and headed out across the water.

"Shall we go?" Ziv asked. "We have very little time. Eben and I will be on the second helicopter. I do not want your mother to get too far ahead of us." He used Angela's shoulder to steady himself as they walked down the stairs.

I turned to Boone. "I have some questions."

"I'm sure you do," Boone said. "But right now I need to talk to the president."

The second helicopter was coming in for a landing.

"After you get off the phone?" I asked.

"We'll be leaving as soon as I finish the conversation. We'll have plenty of time for questions later. Felix is waiting for us in the coach at the cemetery. I need to get you and Angela to San Antonio."

"Are we taking the boat or the helicopter?"

"We'll take the boat."

"Where's Croc?" I hadn't seen him since we left the bedroom.

"He's at the cemetery," Boone said.

"That's what I thought."

Boone smiled and called the president.

On the Road Again

Felix was driving. Croc was in the passenger seat. Boone and Angela and I were sitting at the dining table.

"Kill Devil Hills," Angela said, pointing out the window.

"Odd name," I said.

"Back in the colonial days when a ship foundered, locals would scavenge what they could of the ship's cargo before it sank," Miss Travelogue said. "Sometimes they found rum aboard the ships and they buried it in the sand dunes along here. Back then, rum was called Kill Devil."

That was actually kind of interesting. I felt something vibrating in my pocket. Angela's phone. It was her dad.

I handed it to her. "It's for you."

"Hi Dad . . . Just a second. It's for both of us." She put it on speaker phone.

My mom came on. "Where are you?"

"Kitty Hawk," I said. "Well, actually Kill Devil Hills."

"What are you doing way over there?" Roger asked "I thought you were on your way to Texas."

"We are," Angela said. "Boone figured we had enough time for this detour."

"Wasn't there a hurricane there last night?" Mom asked.

"We got here long after it hit. We're fine."

"I called your phone," Mom said. "You didn't answer."

"I ran out of juice and haven't gotten around to charging it."

"Well, get it charged."

"Will do. How's everything there?"

"Good." Mom said. "We're exhausted, of course, after last night's concert, but we're recovering. The president postponed the press conference, so we're just hanging at the White House."

"The press conference is scheduled for this afternoon," Roger said. "We'll head to Texas as soon as it's over."

"I wish you'd stayed so you could ride on Air Force One," Mom said.

"We probably should have," I said. "But it's been interesting down here. Have you seen the president today?"

"We just had a late breakfast with him and P.K.," Roger said. "They said to say hello to you."

"Tell them hello from us too," Angela said.

"We will," Roger said.

"I guess we better let you go," Mom said. "Love you. Plug in your phone!"

"Okay," I said. *As soon as I get another phone.*

"I love you, sweetheart," Roger said to Angela.

"I love you," Angela answered, and ended the call.

"I wonder if Bethany will show up at the press conference," she said to us.

"That's why the press conference was delayed," Boone said. "J.R. wanted to make sure she was there so the ghost cell would know they had failed."

We passed a McDonalds, which reminded me that I was starving.

"I need to get something to eat," I said.

"And we need gas," Felix said from the driver's seat. "I also want to stop at the Big and Tall Shop. It wasn't open yet when I drove by earlier."

He *did* need a new set of clothes. The ones he had on were in ruins and smelled worse than Croc.

Felix pulled into a gas station next to an outlet mall.

Boone stood. "I'll fill it up."

"I'll do it," Felix said, getting out of the driver's seat. "I need to stretch my legs."

He and Croc stepped out of the coach.

"Where do you want to eat breakfast?" Boone asked.

"Mc–"

"Forget it!" Angela and Boone said in unison.

"It was just an idea," I said. "I don't care where we eat."

"Are you okay?" Angela asked with a grin.

I looked at Boone. "Yes, but I have some questions. How about answering some of them now that we're alone?"

But we weren't alone.

Roger and Mom's bedroom door opened.

Peter "Speed" Paulsen walked out, stifling a yawn.

"Did someone say something about breakfast?" he asked.

About The Author

Born and raised in Portland, Oregon, Roland Smith was just five years old when his parents gave him an old manual typewriter that weighed more than he did, and he's been writing ever since. Now he is the award-winning author of eighteen novels for young readers and more than a dozen nonfiction titles and picture books for children.

Raised in the music business, Smith decided to incorporate that experience as a backdrop for the I, Q series.

When he is not at home writing, Roland Smith spends a good part of the year speaking to students at schools around the country. Learn more about the I, Q books at: www.iqtheseries.com. Learn more about Roland Smith at: www.rolandsmith.com.